ROYAL BASTARDS MC

USA TODAY BESTSELLING AUTHOR
MORGAN JANE MITCHELL

Copyright

Catchin Levi, Royal Bastards MC: Nashville, TN © 2022 Morgan Jane Mitchell

All rights reserved under the International and Pan-American Copyright Conventions. No part of this book may be reproduced or transmitted in any form or by any means, electronic or mechanical, including photocopying, recording, or by any information storage and retrieval system, without permission in writing from the publisher.

This is a work of fiction. Names, places, characters and incidents are either the product of the author's imagination or are used fictitiously, and any resemblance to any actual persons, living or dead, organizations, events or locales is entirely coincidental.

Warning: the unauthorized reproduction or distribution of this copyrighted work is illegal. Criminal copyright infringement, including infringement without monetary gain, is investigated by the FBI and is punishable by up to 5 years in prison and a fine of $250,000.

ISBN: 9798358790643
Imprint: Independently published

www.morganjanemitchell.com

Cover Design: Morgan Jane Mitchell

Model: Alfie Gordillo

Photographer: Steve Kaminsky

ABOUT CATCHIN LEVI

From USA Today Bestselling Author, Morgan Jane Mitchell comes the next installment in her Royal Bastards MC: Nashville, TN, Catchin Levi.

Leviathan is not just any biker, Enforcer for the Royal Bastards MC in Nashville, he's a known **monster**.

What's worse, he's married.

How is Maren, Royal Road's newest dancer, supposed to reel him in? After all, she's deep undercover, bound to catch a killer red handed.

This Halloween as Levi plans his revenge on the rival gang who murdered his sister, Maren thinks she's lured him in.

But Leviathan never met a woman he couldn't capture. At first, Maren's nothing but his bait. However, she awakens his monster, and he claims her as his own.

Entangled in his arms, Maren questions everything she's ever known. When she discovers she's the one who's been caught in the biker's trap, Levi refuses to let her go.
Loving Leviathan comes with a price she never thought she'd be willing to pay. Will she leave his rival gang to be with him?
Will he destroy both their lives just to have her?

STAY UP TO DATE

www.morganjanemitchell.com

ROYAL BASTARDS MC: NASHVILLE, TN CHAPTER

Reading Order

Hallow's Eve (Hallow)

Kissin' Irish (Irish)

Royal Road (Kingpin)

Royal Surprise (Kingpin)

Catchin Levi (Leviathan)

Pagan's X-Mas (Pagan)

Valentines' Eve (TBA)

Royal Pain (Opry)

TBA (Riff)

TBA (Villain)

TBA (Thorn)

TBA (Horror)

ROYAL BASTARDS CODE

PROTECT: The club and your brothers come before anything else, and must be protected at all costs. **CLUB** is **FAMILY**.

RESPECT: Earn it & Give it. Respect club law. Respect the patch. Respect your brothers. Disrespect a member and there will be hell to pay.

HONOR: Being patched in is an honor, not a right. Your colors are sacred, not to be left alone, and **NEVER** let them touch the ground.

OL' LADIES: Never disrespect a member's or brother's Ol'Lady. **PERIOD.**

CHURCH is **MANDATORY.**

LOYALTY: Takes precedence over all, including well-being.

HONESTY: Never **LIE, CHEAT,** or **STEAL** from another member or the club.

TERRITORY: You are to respect your brother's property and follow their Chapter's club rules.

TRUST: Years to earn it, seconds to lose it.

NEVER RIDE OFF: Brothers do not abandon their family.

PROLOGUE

Leviathan

That night the heavens opened and even God wept.

It just started to rain as well. Fat and heavy, droplets fell mounting to a downpour. The shower cooled me as splinters burned my hands. The combination also reminding me of that other awful night. As I tied my Prez's Ol' Lady's blood-soaked body to the makeshift sled, I tried to shake the scene replaying in my mind.

There was no time for nightmares.

We had to get this young lady to the hospital, or she'd be dead too. Securing the wet mess who still breathed, I battled the memories that flooded in. Another tortured, bleeding body kept resurfacing while I stared at this one. The girl before me was no longer Sky, but Leia, my sister who we'd taken off the telephone pole that they used like a cross. The one she'd been nailed to for my sins.

Crucified, my sister's body had merely been a sick message sent from our enemies. They were heartless. They would stop at nothing to punish me for what I did to one of their members. No matter how bad I maimed him, I hadn't killed the fucker. Not for lack of trying, but that's beside the point. What would they expect me to do to the biker who'd been sleeping with my wife for years?

Nevertheless, Leia was long dead by the time we got her down off that post. Once I discovered there was no hope for her, I crashed to my knees. I died. There'd been no greater pain knowing she suffered because of me.

The Asphalt Gods MC had gotten their retribution by killing an innocent soul in the most shocking, excruciating way. Unlike me, my sister, a saint, hadn't deserved it. What's worse, Leia had been with child. I was to be an uncle but became all alone in the world without her. She'd been the only person left of my family who would have anything to do with an outlaw. Leia had been a rare bright spot in this new reality of mine, one of dark and evil shit.

Darkness consumed me afterwards.

It'd been bad enough finding out two of my daughters weren't mine but belonged to another man, a rival club member. But this was worse. All because I beat that biker within an inch of his life, my sister was taken from not just me, but the entire world. Needless to say, I'd never forgive my wife, Chloe. She would forever be dead to me.

And, yeah, after that, with Kingpin in the lead, the Royal Bastards MC ran the Asphalt Gods out of Tennessee. Yet, it wasn't enough for me. It never would be. I yearned for more. They hadn't suffered like I did. I wanted their club to pay a much greater price. I wanted to string up their loved ones, their women like they did my sister. Prez wouldn't have it. He didn't hurt women or children if he could help it. Didn't condone his members doing so either. Fucker suddenly had morals and all that shit.

I settled on killing the men in their club, all of them we could. He agreed, but there was always some excuse to hold off. I wanted to blow up their clubhouse. Prez wanted a plan that would leave our hands clean afterwards. Then he decided that we'd have to be smarter with our vengeance, saying they were simply getting their payback on me to begin with, and they'd do it again. He started saying we couldn't put the Royal Bastards MC members in danger because I wanted my revenge.

"Leia was my sister, Prez. I know you hate your brother. But come on."

"You weren't the only one around here who loved her," Kingpin said, sealing his eyes.

Fuck. If I thought for half a second, they'd come after Leia because of him and not me, I didn't know what I'd do. Would I stoop as low as to kill my President?

Therefore, in the pouring rain as we fought to save my President's Ol' Lady and her unborn child, as he grabbed Memphis's gun from her hand and laid waste to one of the people responsible for this tragedy, a woman, I made up my mind. President or not, I would no longer let him rule me. I'd have my vengeance on the Asphalt Gods MC once and for all, despite the Royal Bastards MC which I'd sworn my allegiance to.

Morgan Jane Mitchell

CHAPTER 1

One Month Earlier

"He's a monster," Paisley said, leaning over the bar. Whore had rainbow hair this week.

No wonder I always felt like she was hitting on me.

With a smirk, she rubbed my arm a little too friendly. "Maren, you are way too beautiful and talented for the likes of Levi." She batted her long pink fake lashes like a toad in a hailstorm.

"Levi?" I asked, yanking my arm out of her reach.

It wasn't that her coming on to me was repulsive. Traveling, I'd witnessed every lifestyle. Nothing bothered me. It was just she reminded me of a clown I fucked in the circus. And here at Royal Road, I learned quickly, Paisley was a low whore on the totem pole. Everyone was on top of her. I wasn't about to catch something in my limited time here.

Were they on such friendly terms that Leviathan had a nickname?

Picking up my drink with the hand I stole from her, I grinned just like when I graced the stage. Like a possum eating sweet potato. Tilting the glass, I sucked down the strawberry margarita and licked the salt from my lips.

The free drinks were the best thing about this place.

Paisley took that as why I drew away from her so quickly. Good. I needed to be liked around here though I was rarely liked anywhere I went.

Strong women usually weren't.

She explained it to me like I was a toddler, "Levi's his for real name. Leviathan is his road name."

"I know all about road names," I said, shaking the ice in my glass to show her I wanted another.

I even had a road name myself, almost.

Paisley refilled my drink. "We get tired of saying Leviathan. It's too damn long if you ask me. Monster or not, he doesn't mind being called Levi. But about anything else will set him off."

"What makes him a monster again?" Though everyone said, no one had expounded on the claim.

Yeah, the biker looked like he'd rip someone in two. I got that much. That only turned me on. Standing about six-five with the build of an athlete, a much larger torso and wingspan, the guy had a presence alright. The menacing tattoos didn't help. Though most of the time, he was clothed. Wearing a t-shirt and jeans with his leather motorcycle vest, he covered up most of his body, of course. And cuts, their colors, I knew about them too. His proudly proclaimed he was the Enforcer of this bunch.

Even so, every inch of his exposed skin was covered in ink. And a time or two I'd watched him coming from the basement where the bikers had a temporary gym since their other one had burned down. Therefore, I'd seen him in his gray sweatpants that were about to fall off.

Holy fuck.

Hovering just over the scrumptious V-shaped muscle diving into his pants, I discovered where those black tentacle tattoos began. Running up his side and barely missing his six-pack, they coated him. Tentacles climbed his large forearms, creeping up his back and biceps to swathe his broad shoulders and thick neck in black ink. They flowed as high as his bald head and encircled it like a cap.

But he wasn't hairless like an old man. Sometimes a slight stubble returned, but the next day his head would be shiny and clean again. So, bald by choice. The same was true of his body and his chin, smooth. Great for me because I never fancied the beard most of the bikers wore in these clubs.

Thankfully, his face was also free of tats. I didn't care for that look either. Reminded me too much of a criminal, like the felons we'd hire on the road to set up our traveling show. But yes, this biker was a criminal, I'd been told.

Although I hadn't seen him smile once, he was absolutely gorgeous in a tough guy way. Plus, there was a glint in his eye that told me he wasn't a simpleton as many strong men were likely to be. At least from afar, since I'd not encountered him yet. And even better, by the looks of him, there was no way in hell he could be over forty. A good thing for me since I was twenty-eight. I didn't like my men being too much older.

Hell. It didn't matter what kind of man I preferred. All I knew was that I had to get close to this monster.

My life depended on it.

"You want to know what made him a monster? Ever since his wife…"

"Fuck, he's married?"

"Yeah, technically. I don't think you'll have any trouble though. He's the cock of this hen house."

He's not faithful? Regardless, that made my mission a lot harder.

"And about him being a monster?" I tried to get her to go on.

"Well, besides him being our Enforcer which means he'd rather kill you than look at ya…."

"He's a murderer?" I interrupted her again, acting shocked. It might be easier than I thought to get something on this biker. "Who has he killed?"

"Is there a Royal Bastard around here who hasn't killed someone?" Paisley said as if manslaughter was a prerequisite to join. However, she quickly changed her tune. "But I don't know all the particulars. That's club business. We're forbidden from speaking about that."

Her "we" meant the sweetbutts, the whores.

"All I know is that the meanest bikers in this club shake in their boots at the mere mention of getting on Leviathan's shit list. That's enough for me."

"Is that all?" I dug in my bowl of nuts for a spicy one and popped it in my mouth.

Taking in a breath, Paisley lifted her shoulders and dropped them, dramatically. She was giving in.

"Leviathan is ruthless, basically. There's no line he won't cross. Like Kingpin, our Prez is very reluctant to even strike a woman. He has Memphis keep us in line around here. For him to do something to a woman, she'd have to have done something atrocious. Outside of the bedroom that is. Pagan, our VP has a soft spot for his blind sister and doesn't do much that would truly bother her or endanger her. Nothing he'd let her find out about at least. Levi has no such rules for himself anymore, not since his sister died. He's pure evil. All he thinks about is killing this one or that one. Which makes him even worse in the sack, rough and uncaring. If you plan on taking him to bed, take some Tylenol first."

"Yikes," I said, although just the thought of it turned me on.

"And it's not just for the bruises he'll give you. Man is hung like a pizza."

"You mean a horse?"

"No, a large pizza. Sixteen inches."

"That's impossible."

"Well, I know that, but a horse doesn't do it justice. Believe me."

"How about a moose?"

"What am I fucking Canadian? I've never seen a moose's wang. I'm sticking with a large pizza. We sweetbutts have a scale around here. We've done run out of animals."

"You've been with Leviathan?"

"Once, but it was ages ago. Too much pizza for me." Her eyes got wide to convey her message.

I got it. "Well, what does he like?" If I was going to catch this gigantic fish, I needed to know what lure to use.

"Maren, you really are too good for him. For God's sake, you've got it made here at Royal Road. I've heard you've not turned any tricks. You think everyone's so impressed with your exotic dances no one expects you to entertain our guests after hours," Paisley complained.

"No. I've not been with anyone."

I would add I wasn't a whore, but it would offend her. And it'd blow my cover. Royal Road might not be your average MC clubhouse, but it was still a meat market.

Nevertheless, I did hold out my hands, explaining, "I was hired strictly for my act. Not as a stripper. Opry said everything else was optional."

He also said I'd be compensated well if I chose to take the bikers or the high rollers to my bed.

"Opry always says that. He has to. Guess things have changed." Paisley crossed her arms and stuck out her bottom lip. She didn't seem incredibly happy about it.

"Wasn't always like this?"

"Our Prez took an Ol' Lady," she declared like it was the end of the world, like it explained everything.

That was what the bikers called their wives, Ol' Ladies. And I knew her President recently married. It was the talk of the club.

"I'm sure you heard. And Memphis, the bombshell blonde over there is his ex."

I tracked her gaze to see the stripper completely naked on the stage. Bent over, she showed off her cooter and pooter at once. I knew of her, too.

"She's one of his exes. Anyway, she used to manage us sweetbutts. Memphis made sure we all understood what our guests expected here at Royal Road. If you're on the payroll, you play ho, was her motto. You were hired just as she decided that wasn't her job anymore."

Thank God.

Paisley wagged a pointed nail at me. "But don't think it's going to last. Sweet Tea wants to step up and keep us in line. She's been here in the evenings, putting in extra hours hoping to get Opry's attention."

"Thanks for the warning. Back to Levi." I tried on his real name.

"Girl, you don't want to mess with him."

The whore didn't know how wrong she was. Not only would I have to mess with him, hearing how dangerous he was did nothing but excite me.

Downing my new drink, I crunched the ice. Then I turned my back on her. I was done. She was useless.

That got her to talk.

"Maren, wait."

I spun back to her. Resting an elbow on the bar, I propped my chin up on a hand, waiting.

"You don't have to do much to attract him. I've seen him watching your performances." She rolled her eyes, clearly not appreciating the art of contortion. "Watching you in general. Not sure why he hasn't made his move yet."

Oh, I hadn't noticed. "Are you sure?"

"Yes, man's drooling. Trust me. There's nothing that gets past me when it comes to this club. You've done something to him."

"I've not given him the time of day."

Hell, I hadn't given any men any attention. I'd only done my act, a seductive contortionist's display, all done topless, but not bottomless like most of the strippers here. And I've not fallen for any of the biker's advancements. Not just that, I'd escaped them completely, but that wouldn't always be the case.

The men who patronized this place were too scared to upset a whore and earn the wrath of their biker pimps. You could tell them to get lost if you felt like it. But the club members didn't usually take no for an answer. So far, I'd lucked out, having plenty of whores around to pawn the bikers off on. Naturally, I hung out with all the other girls, so I could direct all the men who wanted me someone else's way.

Eventually, my luck would run out. I was playing with fire because I might get burnt.

"Whatever you're doing it's working," Paisley said with a bow, like she was impressed.

That was good to know. Basically, I'd set my trap. After all, I was deep undercover trying to catch this killer red-handed. Once I lured Leviathan in, got him attached to me, really attached, I'd tell him I was a spy for his most hated enemy, a rival biker gang, the Asphalt Gods MC.

Yes, the cruelty of it was the point.

I had my orders.

The monster would make his move. He'd try to kill me. Once that happened, I was to call the Gods to descend on Royal Road to massacre all the Royal Bastards here.

Anything to earn my patch.

I only hoped I survived.

The bikers all noticed the new dancer who wasn't attached to anyone. They were all pestering me. I couldn't go after Leviathan first off because that would be too suspicious. Hell, I'd waited well over a month to even ask about him.

Querying Paisley about the biker would cause her to run and tell everyone I had the hots for him. Whore was nothing if not a gossip. This place was all too obvious. I'd figured it out in no time.

I'd catch Levi sooner rather than later, but I'd have to swat all the other flies away first. It'd be much easier if he would come to me already. When he did, I'd be the girl with eyes only for him. Men were easy. But would the wife be a problem?

As it was, I was going to have to pick another biker to succumb to first as to not seem questionable. The sad one whose girl just stood him up at the altar would do. He'd been working his way through all the women here for a while now.

Next week I found myself on my knees in the dressing room with Hallow's dick in my mouth.

CHAPTER 2

I stood at the door to the Throne Room, my arms crossed. The damn thing automatically locked, but our Prez liked the appearance of security when there was a crowd at Royal Road. And there was a huge mob tonight. There was almost nothing I despised more than a packed clubhouse. It spelled trouble. And trouble would be my problem. I didn't want to be here, and Kingpin, our President didn't want me here either. Even if I was his Enforcer, I wasn't his first choice for the job. However, Goliath had been strangely unavailable lately.

At least I enjoyed the show that attracted such a horde. That was until a biker blocked my view. He chewed on a toothpick as always.

"Leviathan, glad you're back," Opry said, tipping his cowboy hat.

He wasn't my boss, but he managed the business side of Royal Road. And I'd been back for a while now, but I didn't count on him to notice. He'd been busy dicking some young new stripper. He went through them like water.

"I see you like the new dancer I hired."

I waited for it. The cowboy winked. The man was predictable.

23

"What makes you say that?" I asked as I moved to see past him, to see her.

"You can't seem to take your eyes off her," he said, joining me against the door.

We watched her together.

He was right. My gaze hadn't left Maren since she took the stage. She'd caught my eye the first night she performed.

Amongst the sleaze Royal Road offered we had a few decent acts. Our live music counted as one. Maren's act proved to be another showstopper. The blonde adorned our stage in a shimmering dress that barely covered her smoking body. That was nothing new around the club, women with hot bods.

Maren's attire wasn't just provocative, it was theatrical. She wore her platinum hair up, embellished with a crown and jewels. Rhinestones covered her body in strategic places, highlighting her shoulders, her wrists, her navel. And she didn't just twerk and pretend to fuck the pole.

Opry had gone all out, hanging a swing for her. Stretching her silky leg to the sky, she embraced the rope with her foot, twirling it around her ankle. Like magic, she threaded her body through the hoop, flipping around it like a fish out of water. Seductively, she hung from it, weaving herself into beautiful incredible postures. And just when you couldn't believe your eyes, she'd remove her top and floor you with the best set of tits I'd ever had the privilege to see.

Fuck, yeah.

When she did so, her fingers hesitated on her neck before trailing the curves of her bosom. With anguish, she displayed her body. Tormented, she became vulnerable where the other women here became sluts. The dancer didn't go any further, taking anything else off. However, the show took an intense, suggestive turn. Her movements more exaggerated, her features turned to pure sex. The woman's body morphed into a piece of erotic art.

Maren changed up her finale like she did her costume. Then her act would take a lighter turn. She'd start into a belly dance to close out the show. Once she lit a torch aflame with her toes, wrenched it up to her mouth and swallowed it. There was always something new. The babe kept us all on the edge of our seats.

Tonight, she danced with sharp swords, somehow engulfing them too. You could hear a pin drop. The long metal disappearing in her throat made me hold my breath until she heaved it out. And I could hold my breath for an exceptionally long time.

When I could breathe again, I exhaled, "Fuck, yeah, Opry. Who doesn't like this shit."

The other bikers were mesmerized, too. We all had to be imagining what we could do to a girl who could move like that. I knew I was. We all wanted her to swallow our swords. The crowd here loved it as well. Applause boomed as she headed off stage to the dressing room.

I'd heard the whores were all jealous that Opry hired someone with true talent to dance for once. The lights changed with the music. When the strippers came out and started to take it all off, no one was too impressed anymore. The drinking, the chatter and the sound of the slot machines resumed.

"Just checking," Opry explained, like our deep concentration on the girl's show hadn't interrupted our conversation. "Didn't want to make a move on Maren if you were going for it."

Going for it? "Isn't she a bit too old for you? What happened to that nineteen-year-old who's been warming your bed?" The girl practically lived with him.

"Leo? She's a handful. A PITA."

"Speak English, brother."

"Exactly. That means she's a pain in the ass. I like them young, but the language has changed. I can barely understand her sometimes."

"What are you doing talking to her?"

"Some of us need more than pussy, Levi. That Maren seems like she'd be real interesting in the hay and otherwise."

"Need a girl to entertain you, Opry? Man, you are getting old."

He sniffed. "Your hair would be gray if you didn't shave it all off."

Just then his girl, Leo stepped onto the stage. She didn't need to strip. In five-inch pink stilettos, she was already naked but had sprayed on a whipped cream bikini. It'd either melt off and fall off as she slid up and down the pole. The whores were doing anything they could to compete with Maren's show, but Leo was the more ridiculous of the bunch.

"She seems pretty entertaining, brother," I told him, watching her slip on the cream and fall on her ass.

Opry made a face, and I could tell he'd grown tired of her.

"About Maren?" he asked.

"What about her?"

I'd been watching her, but not just her act. I recognized her, had seen her somewhere before. But I couldn't place her. Opry said she was from the area, so it was possible. I didn't usually forget a beautiful woman. However, there was something more. She didn't seem like she belonged at Royal Road.

"Are you going to do something about it? Paisley says the girl's been asking about you," he admitted.

"She has?" I asked quickly, giving my interest away, something I didn't intend to do.

"Yep. Asking how you are in bed and shit like that. They've been talking about that monster in your pants."

"Paisley wouldn't know."

"I know you've made your way through the sweetbutts. I've not seen Maren with anyone else. Memphis isn't exactly keeping them in line."

"You expect Maren to whore herself out?"

"She's on the payroll, ain't she?"

"Maren's different. She's like Eve." I spoke of another talented performer at Royal Road, a singer, someone I didn't care for on account of her ties to our rival club. "Eve's not expected to be available."

"Don't be so sure. Eve was taken. But she's not Hallow's girl anymore. Up for the taking now."

"You don't be so sure," I warned him.

The whores all thought they knew what happened at Royal Road, but they didn't know the half of it. Prez had nothing but trouble with his new wife because she thought he had something going on with Eve. I wasn't entirely sure the biker didn't want the songstress. Man had taken an unusual liking to her, taking her under his wing. He sure as fuck wouldn't have saved her life from my wrath for her to be Hallow's woman.

Speaking of the devil, I saw Hallow the next night. I was free of Kingpin, so I went to go find Maren before she took the stage. Before Opry got to her. It was time I introduced myself.

Cracking open the door, I couldn't believe what I saw.

CHAPTER 3

Leaving the dressing room, I wiped the corners of my mouth. Seducing that biker had been way too easy, and I didn't even have to fuck him. He'd been too drunk to perform anyway. Hopefully not too smashed to go forth and tell of his exploits, if only to hurt his ex-fiancée.

Little did he know, I was the one to break his heart last month. I alerted my President, Killer of the Asphalt Gods MC in Arkansas about Hallow's woman, Eve, contacting her brother at my club. Afterwards, her brother had to fetch her from Royal Road, making her leave Hallow on their wedding day. I also called my boss and told him about the Royal Bastards' President's new bride too. At the time I hadn't heard she was pregnant, but the walls had ears and the whores talked.

Even if Hallow was too intoxicated to remember, I'd tell the whores myself that I sucked him dry. Leviathan would hear about me finally being with someone in this club, sort of. And that I had my eye on him as well. Seemed a man never wanted you until you were with someone else.

A smile burned on my face, knowing my trap was set. My plans were working. The danger grew. Biting my lip, suddenly, I regretted not taking that biker to my bed over the clubhouse. I'd been here over a month already and hadn't had any sex. At a biker club like this, I should be having a smorgasbord of partners, but my mission didn't call for it. My mission was to make a monster fall very much in love with me and break his heart. I was poking a hornet's nest, and it thrilled me.

"What's your deal?" a voice boomed next to me.

Fucking shit. He scared the crap out of me. I jumped like a cartoon cat.

Standing right outside the dressing room, Leviathan waited for me.

That was quick.

By the look on his face, I guess he'd been watching. The biker hadn't spoken a word to me before, the whole time I'd been here. Up close, he was even larger and much more scrumptious. To me, Leviathan dripped with raw sex appeal. But everyone here feared him. I supposed a girl could fall in love with the devil if she didn't know all his sins.

"I could ask you the same thing. Were you spying on me?" I accused him.

"What if I had been?"

"Did you like what you saw?"

Dressed for my act, I was practically naked. Leviathan was too covered for my liking.

The biker shook his head. "No, seriously. Who are you?"

"What's it to you?"

"I take my job seriously. You're not getting along with any of the bikers here, and then all the sudden you're on your knees for Hallow of all people," Leviathan said, the suspicion evident in his tone.

"You mean, I'm not fucking anyone. Is that a crime? Is sucking a dick a crime?"

He leered. "If it's not mine, maybe it is. I know you ain't attracted to no sloppy drunk."

"How do you know? Have you been watching me?" I wanted to know if Paisley was right.

"A little whore whispered it in my ear."

The whore was quick with her gossip, too.

"Is this your way of coming on to me?" I asked with a sly grin. I fluttered my eyes like Paisley had at me, like they might take flight.

"I'm curious what a girl's doing at Royal Road if she's not got a biker between her thighs. At least want one. Or a few. From what I hear, your bed's staying empty even though you're on the payroll."

My whole face puckered up. "I'm not a girl. I'm a woman. I know you bikers like them young so maybe y'all don't like me."

"Bullshit. What are you, twenty-five? Young enough for most of these geezers."

"I'm working. Excuse me," I said, pushing past him, but making sure to rub my body on him as I did.

The biker seized my shoulders, stopping me. He twirled me to face him like I was nothing.

"Who are you?" he asked again, his voice lower. His enormous hands ran down my arms.

"Get your paws off me," I struggled to get loose.

With that the biker only got closer. He wrapped his arms around me and there was no way I could move an inch. He smelled of leather and whiskey, mixed with his natural manly musk. A calloused hand snaked around my bare midriff to my back sending shivers all over my skin. With his firm grip, he secured me. The body heat radiating off him alone caused an instant sweat, but I was burning up for another reason. I fell against the Python in his jeans. The biker's erection practically beat against my thigh like it had a lifeforce of its own.

Fuck me. Sincerely. Literally just fuck me. Right now. I fought the urge to scream it aloud.

"Who are you?" Leviathan growled this time.

Good gracious. I'd turned into goo. As I melted against him, I tried to keep the infatuated look off my face.

"Tell me." He shook me, like he could shake it out of me.

Oh, my, his dick rocked against me. I dug my nails into him, but not to deter him. I was about to lose it. Sucking in a breath, I held it so I wouldn't give myself away.

He didn't budge. "Now," he demanded, his voice sexy as all get out.

Oh, I was exactly who I said I was when applying at Royal Road. I told the manager who hired me I was an ex-gymnast who had aged out of competing. An ex-circus performer who had traveled the country. One who suffered an injury bad enough to keep me off the road. Maren's my for real name too. Told the biker running this joint all I needed was a hoop hanging from the ceiling and the right lighting, and I could give these outlaws a show to remember. Opry informed me Royal Road was much more than a biker bar, that he needed someone like me, a true entertainer for his more refined guests, his high rollers who filled their coffers.

"After all, this is Nashvegas," he'd said. "Could use a contortionist."

"Heard you were a carnie. Tell me about that," Leviathan snickered, interrogating me. "Traveling?" But all the while he sniffed me and felt me up like a wild animal.

My hands soared to his vast chest to push him away. Though I played repulsed, I was eating his touch up.

"Yeah, I was a performer with a cirque style entertainment company. Real upstanding place where we weren't called carnies for crying out loud."

"Doing what?"

"Flying trapeze, mostly."

The peril had been a rush, addictive. The start of all my troubles.

"Not contortion?"

"Only on the side. I'm not flexible enough to compete with the other performers."

"Seem pretty good at it."

"To a layman's eyes, yeah."

Leviathan licked his lips. "The way you twist into a pretzel… The things I could do to you in that position."

"Like I haven't heard that one before."

"But have you done it?"

I gulped. "That's not why I'm here, to let bikers fuck me in weird positions."

"Hell, by the look of it, you could lick my balls while I fucked you."

That warranted an eye roll. "If you only knew what I could do to a man you'd be a lot nicer."

Leviathan took that as a cue to get meaner. His fingernails dug into my arms this time. "Why are you here? Why did you leave the circus?"

"Why do you care?"

"I'm asking the questions."

I glared at his hand that squeezed my arm though he practically had me in an embrace. "Is this a date? Do you want to get to know me?" I asked him.

"If it was a fucking date, you'd know it." The man almost smiled but in a menacing way.

Good golly. I liquefied again.

"Why so serious?" I asked and chuckled a bit at myself.

The big guy didn't give an inch. "Tell me, and I might just let you suck my dick next."

"So, you were watching me."

"I didn't like what I saw," he said, his voice so husky.

"You think this will convince me to give up other bikers for you?"

Leviathan steered my arm behind my back, actually hurting me for a moment.

A rush zipped through me. I couldn't let him know how much I enjoyed it. The chance I might be hurt. Thankfully, he eased up, so he didn't break my arm.

"Are you going to tell me what the fuck you're doing at Royal Road?"

I squeaked out, "Listen. At twenty-one I aged out of gymnastics. Before you ask, you wouldn't understand. I was good. So good, I almost went to the Olympics as a teen. But my body ached all over most days. I got burnt out. Too old for the sport, I could still dance, only on the ground. My coach had me audition for a traveling show way out in Oklahoma. They liked me, and I didn't have anything else to fall back on. I barely graduated high school. Yes, an RV became my home. We had appearances all over the US. I had some fun at first. Before I fell. They kept me on as a trainer, then a manager, and it turned into a lot of work. I got burnt out at the circus, too. I moved back home. I used to live in this area. Why wouldn't I come to Royal Road? I needed a job. Money."

That last part was a lie. I was from Arkansas although I'd been in Tennessee often enough as a teen to compete in gymnastics. The rest of my story was mostly true. The best way to lie was hidden in a whole lot of truths and within too much information. The more someone thought they knew, the more they'd believe. That was something I learned on the road.

What I didn't tell Leviathan was that in my time in the circus, my love of the trapeze morphed into a love of danger. No. A bad addiction. And yes, with stage makeup, choreography, I made up characters. I had stage characters galore. I'd used them all over the country and in Arkansas at the Asphalt Gods MC clubhouse. None bigger than Spooky, my road name there, if I were to be patched. Unlike this motorcycle club, they patched women, made them members.

But Spooky was not who I was at the moment. I knew to pull off this trick, I'd have to be myself, simply Maren. I couldn't be caught in a lie. The circus performer, Maren put an element of danger in all her acts unlike here at Royal Road where the seduction was solely the point of her routines. My routines.

By the way Levi spoke of fucking me as a pretzel, they'd hooked him.

My mission was the danger now, the danger of catching Leviathan in the act of trying to kill me. Once he found out I was his enemy. After he fell for me, of course, and I revealed my true identity.

He's a monster. A murderer, Killer had told me. He'd exterminate any Asphalt Gods MC member he could catch for some reason. He'd massacre us all if he had the chance.

I was simply Killer's beautiful bait.

What Opry didn't know when he hired me was that I'd gone to the Asphalt Gods MC first. I became a dancer for their small club, but I rode with them too, became a prospect. Craving danger above all, being a member of a one-percenter motorcycle club appealed to me like nothing else. Killer, their President was so impressed he proclaimed I could use my skills for something else. As a probate I didn't have a choice but to obey my President. I had the job of seducing a monster, no question.

Well, there were actually two options. I'd either succeed and earn my patch or I'd die trying, at the hands of one club or another.

My situation was precarious as can be.

"Just a job?" Leviathan wasn't convinced.

"It's the truth," I added.

The monster smiled, and my world crumbled.

Hell.

Pretending to be in love wouldn't be hard at all.

"I think I know you," he said, shocking the hell out of me.

CHAPTER 4

Maren

"Know me?" That's impossible... I started to say but then I remembered I claimed to be from the Nashville area. I plastered on my own smile. "How do you think you know me?"

Leviathan released me partly, pointed a thumb at himself. "You competed in the Olympics the year I went. Well, I almost competed."

"The Olympics?" Was he for real?

"Yeah, you were young. Way younger than me, still in school. Maren Davidson. I remember your name on the roster because I really loved Harleys, even back then."

That was me alright. The fucker did know of me.

"I didn't end up going, either. That was a lifetime ago. I was sixteen. My mom got nervous about it. She wouldn't fly, and she said there were too many perverts around. I never got that close to qualifying again. Not that I didn't try. Little did I know that would be my last shot."

I didn't remember him being an Olympic hopeful that year, but I was so young. Maybe he was pulling my leg.

"Yeah, I was twenty six. Already too old, so my last shot too. I got banned that year. From swimming."

I slapped my hand over my mouth, reacting. "Oh, I'm sorry."

There was no denying he had the physique of a swimmer. I fought the urge to roll my eyes at his tattoos that took on a whole new and obvious meaning now. Evidently, he wasn't lying.

"It was nothing," he blew it off.

"Drugs?" I guessed, teasing him.

"No," he said in such a defensive way, he clearly didn't want to talk about it. Then he softened, surprising me. He answered, "Sexual harassment."

"Oh." I made a face before I caught myself.

"Yeah, I was who your mother warned you about. No, I mean, that's what everyone thought. One of the lady coaches had a thing for me, older lady. Older than me back then in her forties. She threatened me. I gave into her, fucked her, and ended up suffering the consequences anyway."

"How did you end up here?"

"Same as you really. Had to use all this muscle for something. Besides, that coach was jealous of my real girl. Bitch found out I had a baby mama back home and wanted to ruin my life. She did."

"Then you turned to motorcycles and crime?"

"Not at first. My wife's older brother had been part of this club. Soon as I got banned, fucker threatened my life. He said I had to finally make an honest woman of her and join up since I'd lost my career. I agreed. Had nothing else going for me anyway. He's since passed, but here I am, still one of these Bastards."

"You didn't love her, your wife?"

"We had a four-year-old together. Seemed like the right thing to do at the time."

"But you're still married?" I asked, clearly asking something more since I was pressed against his dick that pulsated through his pants.

"Yeah, still married. But it won't keep me out of your bed," he promised with a simper.

Before I could play like I didn't want him there, someone cleared their throat beside us.

Sweet Tea stood with her hands on her hips.

"Why ain't you on stage?" she barked at me.

Hell, was it time for me to go on? I'd lost track.

Leviathan hadn't stirred, he still held me against his substantial erection.

"We're not finished here, Sweet Tea," he said, like he had the upper hand. "Maren has somewhere to be. She's not performing tonight."

Holy moly. He meant I'd be with him. I was putty in his hands.

"Levi, put your dick back in your pants. You're needed too. I'm just a messenger. Pagan's looking for you. Club business."

Pagan was the Vice President and the only man beside his President who Levi answered to. At that he simply let go of me. He left like nothing had happened.

Frustrated, I watched him walk away.

Sweet Tea noticed the dreamy look on my face. She warned, "Watch yourself. That man will break you."

"Don't worry about me," I said. "I'm tough."

"I don't mean your heart. That biker's dick's the size of a Mac Truck."

"You been with him too? I thought it was a large pizza."

"Paisley's always using the absurd food scale she made up, when we already got a perfectly good road scale. Take Pagan, he's a wood paneled station wagon from the seventies cause he's big, but he's all hippyish. No manscaping to be found. You'll be going to the woods with that one. Our Prez, he's a monster truck, larger than life, loud paint. You might've seen one, but you'll never own one. Dick destroys everything. Levi's a Mac Truck. You can drive it, but you need a whole distinct set of credentials. Some training. And he's dangerous, more interested in running you down than driving. But when he does get in the right gear, he likes you skinny girls. Toothpicks. Likes splitting you toothpicks."

"I'm so not a toothpick," I said, laughing at the thought and her wild comparisons. I was heavier and curvier than most of the girls here, but that wasn't saying much. Most of them were stick creatures. "Sweet Tea, you're gorgeous."

She huffed like she didn't believe me.

I was being genuine. She had enough meat on her to make her truly attractive, in my opinion. She wore it well and looked like she could kick someone's ass. I didn't want to get on her bad side.

"I know I'm more than a snack but honey, some men can't handle me. But I remind Levi too much of his wife. Wait 'til Chloe hears about you. She's going to stick her boot up your ass."

"Why me? Everyone says he sleeps with, well, everyone around here."

"Yeah, but they all hoes. You've not taken any clients the whole time you've been here, so not a hoe yet. Now monstrous Levi's seen hugged up on you. Biker doesn't do PDA. The way I see it, he must've been the reason you've not been with any other men. His girl's gonna stomp your lights out. She don't want to lose him. They done got three kids together."

"Three kids?" Oh, yeah. He said he had a kid with the girl he married. But three? I hadn't even had time to think about what that meant. Levi had kids. Why hadn't anyone told me? Killer sure as hell hadn't mentioned it when he sent me to lure the man to his death.

"Three daughters, the oldest one sixteen now, if you can believe it. The other two are a lot younger."

I tried using everything I'd learned to calculate in my head but failed. I asked her since she seemed to know everything., "How old is Leviathan?"

"Thirty-nine."

I'd been right, under forty. Not that it mattered. I had a mission. I'd made progress, but I didn't see him again that night.

As I sat in the hoop that hung over the stage at Royal Road, installed for me, I watched for the big guy. He was hard to miss and nowhere to be seen as I twisted into impossible, seductive poses. All to lure him in.

After the show, I searched some more to no avail. I went to bed alone thinking of all the people I'd met over the last month that would die because of me, and kids maybe. What the hell was I doing? Who would I harm in my quest for danger? Afterall, that was why I became a prospect and ended up on this mission in the first place.

I thought he'd been wanting to take me to his bed, like he said, but I didn't see Leviathan again all week. The biker was always gone. He was supposed to be Kingpin's Enforcer, but he was barely around. Another biker guarded their President.

Taking my morning stroll, I walked past the row of houses for the officers, wanting to somehow run into him. I wondered if he was gone with his wife and kids. Though, I didn't want to chase him. And when I did see him show up like magic the next week, he was preoccupied.

When I felt like I might have to do something more drastic, like text the man, since Paisley had given me his number, we met briefly completely by accident.

I woke up starving, staggered down the stairs like a zombie, filled a plate from the buffet on autopilot and sat at the bar before the early show. To compete with the tourist trap of Broadway in Nashville, Royal Road's shows started at two in the afternoon.

Levi asked if I needed some coffee.

"Yeah, I'm useless without it," I said before I even realized I'd taken a seat beside him.

Morgan Jane Mitchell

CHAPTER 5

Maren

The biker went behind the bar and poured me a cup. He asked how I liked it.

"Bitter but sweet, like I like my men."

Sitting the cup down in front of me, he slid the sugar to me.

I set it aside and grabbed a packet of the artificial stuff.

Levi sat back beside me. An empty plate in front of him, he'd finished eating. With him next to me, I could barely start. We listened to Eve who practiced on the stage without her band. She sang Loretta Lynn's, "Don't Come Home a Drinking".

"She found out about you, yet?" he asked as soon as I took a bite.

I'd almost forgotten I'd had her man, Hallow's dick in my mouth the other week. My hand over my mouth, I chewed the chewiest bacon I'd ever had.

"Don't know or don't care," I answered as soon as I swallowed it.

"How's that? Folks say y'all are friends." Levi was still trying to figure me out.

"We are," I lied. Picking up the coffee, I washed the bacon out of my teeth.

I guess it looked like we were friends. I talked to her and everyone else here a plenty. It's not that the women around here weren't nice and all, but I couldn't get attached.

I changed the subject. "It's just, I'm more worried about your wife. Sweet Tea said she'd hurt me if I got close to you. I should probably steer clear then. That's why you haven't seen me around." I played like I'd been gone too.

"Chloe? Don't worry about her. I didn't want to miss your shows last week, but I've been gone myself. Club business."

That was all the bikers' excuse around here.

Abruptly, Kingpin busted into the club holding a gift-wrapped box and hollered for everyone to leave. He disappeared into his office. That biker was a whirlwind. Fuck that, he was a damn tornado. When the King spoke, everyone listened. And I wasn't talking about the old biker who had been an Elvis impersonator who sang here sometimes. Their MC President had spoken.

Levi stood at attention. Sweet Tea, took off her apron and slammed it down on the counter, complaining, but she went and shut the buffet table. Eve nearly dropped her mike and exited the stage. The small crowd of members that didn't join Kingpin in his office filtered out from all exits. There hadn't been many since it was before noon.

Something was going on, therefore that meant Levi had to leave too.

Showing me that rare smile again, he took my hand and kissed it before he left. The gesture hadn't at all gone with his tough persona. I felt smitten for a moment until another biker approached me.

"Get on out," Riff came, shooing me away. Road Captain, he acted like the boss of everyone.

At least I had the night off, but I didn't see Leviathan later when Royal Road opened again to the public. Was I the only one to notice he was gone all the time?

I decided to ask Sky, the President's Ol' Lady.

She was a goth as him. Just as mysterious. She sat at the bar with her best friend Leo, a mixed girl with an ass like a dump truck. Well, they were cousins somehow, though one was just some white girl with her hair dyed jet-black, and one was darker skinned, with bleached caramel blonde waves down to her ass crack.

Leo resembled a young and beautiful Mariah Carey with a much larger ass. She stripped like no one's business and fucked our direct superior, Opry. A biker who donned a cowboy hat and matching boots like he belonged out on a ranch roping cattle. Talked like it too. The man who hired me was twenty years her senior. There wasn't as big of an age gap between Levi and me.

Younger than me by quite a few years, the girls were both on about something as usual. Habitually, Sky thought her new husband banged everyone in the club. Pregnancy did that

49

to women, I heard. The whores were no help, taking joy in feeding her fears. But MC presidents weren't known for keeping faithful. So, perhaps she was onto something.

Nevertheless, I certainly didn't care.

I took a seat with them, a forlorn look on my face.

"Who shittled on your rainbow?" Leo asked in her usual tactless manner.

I would never live down confessing to them I'd been with a woman before. That was way before I discovered I liked dick best. Folks around here weren't as open minded as me.

"Leave her alone. She's looking for Levi. He's not been coming in," Paisley butted in from behind the bar. "He's like that. Hit it and quit it."

"Probably with his wife," I said, fishing. "And I've not hit anything."

Sky answered, "No, he's helping Kingpin put out fires. Not literal ones this time."

Someone else was behind the bar. "Memphis is causing problems," Cece told us.

Everyone fell silent. You didn't talk about Memphis in front of Sky. The girl's face turned blood red at the mention of her name.

Cece went on, "What? I might be blind, but anyone could see that. She's pissed Kingpin is in love for once."

Sky smiled, and everyone blew out a breath.

"Isn't Prez performing tonight? With Eve," Paisley said.

They all got quiet again.

Cece chirped, "Sky, I thought you two were headed to the cabin for a real honeymoon?"

Leo shook her head, trying to stop the girl from mentioning it, but the poor thing was blind and couldn't see her.

Good God. I wanted to run far away from this drama. I excused myself as the show started.

Levi appeared out of nowhere.

"Come with me," he said.

Reaching out his hand, he led me out front to his motorcycle.

"Do you ride?"

"No," I lied.

"You ever rode bitch?"

"No," I answered. That was the truth.

"Well, then you'll have to be my bitch, tonight." He winked like no one's business. "I'm supposed to go check out a rival club."

My heart stopped. Had I been found out? Was he going to the Asphalt Gods MC clubhouse? What would I do? I was dead.

"Headed to a strip club named Shakey's. You coming?"

Fucking hell. I resurrected.

"Prez is worried about something going on there."

"I'm not sure I'm dressed for it."

I didn't have on the skimpy outfit I performed in, but I'd dressed for a night at Royal Road. I wasn't exactly wearing much clothing. Nothing close to what I'd pick out for a ride on a motorcycle.

In the miniskirt, I worried about sitting on the bike. Not only was my cleavage on display, but my arms were also. Fuck, I'd be frozen by the time we got there. Besides, I'd never been on a motorcycle in heels like I wore this evening. I wasn't that talented. And I've never ridden on the back with a man before. I longed for my leathers, my boots, and my own Harley.

Leviathan slouched off his leather jacket.

"Here, wear this so you don't freeze."

"Is it safe for me to go check this out with you?" I asked him, putting on his coat that swallowed me whole.

Warm, it smelled like him. I breathed it in, relishing the scent. And the weight of it reminded me of being squeezed by his massive arms just last week. His eyes ran up and down me. He grinned like he liked seeing me in his big jacket.

"No. Nothing is ever safe with me," he answered me finally, all serious.

"You'll have to protect me," I said, playing like I couldn't take care of myself.

Levi stepped in close. "I won't let you out of my sight."

I hopped on the back of his Harley and spread my legs out so he could take his seat.

Sliding in front of me, Levi started the bike. The engine roared and vibrated, sending shudders through me. Oh, how I'd missed it.

"Hold on tight." He had to remind me since I'd never been on the back before.

I wrapped my arms around this dangerous man. Running my hands up under his cut, I pressed my cheek into his club's logo and hooked my thumbs into his belt loops.

Morgan Jane Mitchell

Morgan Jane Mitchell

CHAPTER 6

Maren

Ignoring the speed limit, Leviathan's motorcycle raced through Nashville. The biker hadn't played it safe on my behalf. The ride alone had been dangerous, exhilarating. We ended up in front of a rundown building just off the interstate. A cheap neon sign flashed, Shakey's. Bodiless legs danced beneath. The universal symbol for a strip club if you will.

"I'm sure you've heard of this place. Being from the area and all," Leviathan said as soon as I could hear him. He still doubted me.

"Of course. Most of the girls at Royal Road used to work here."

"But not you?"

"No."

Levi took my waist and practically pulled me off his bike. "I'm checking something out. But we can enjoy the show. You understand?"

"Okay?"

"You're with me," he said, taking my hand.

Levi took me inside as if I was his date. I played along. I sort of was his date, wearing his motorcycle jacket and all. We'd hit it off.

Inside the place was depressing. Nothing like the grandness of Royal Road. Leviathan shrugged off all the glares. The men knew him but avoided him at all costs. Not the women though. They started to come our way, but once they saw me, they backed off.

Sitting in front of the stage, he ordered us drinks.

"What do you want?"

"A strawberry margarita on the rocks."

"You always drink that, why?"

He'd been watching me. "Started in Galveston, Texas. When I started in the circus. I miss it."

"You said Oklahoma." He tried to catch me in a lie.

"Yes, Oklahoma is where we were based, but this margarita started in Texas when we had a show there."

"You ever think of going back?"

"To the circus? No. I'll never travel again like that. But I have no roots. So yeah, I'd love to live in Texas. If I had a choice."

"Why don't you have a choice?"

Skewing my lips, I caught myself. I almost told him I'd made a huge mistake, prospecting with a mean ass motorcycle club and I was in over my head. But that it also intrigued me, thrilled me. "I just go where life takes me," I recovered, realizing how dumb that sounded.

We watched the strippers who were much tamer than at Royal Road. Levi seemed to enjoy it. Spreading his legs, he leaned back so the action could grow in his jeans. Looked like that alien from the movie was about to bust out of his zipper. I imagined his dick dancing off with a top hat and cane and knew I had my movies seriously confused with cartoons.

My drink arrived and I slammed it back quick. Levi ordered me another. He put his arm around me as he sucked down a beer, but he was distracted. He was looking for someone. Clearly, I was part of his cover. It didn't stop him from suddenly leaning in and placing kisses down my neck.

Oh, wow.

His hand went to my thigh, inching up my short skirt. My stomach twisted as I longed for him. An ache filled me where he should be.

His lips faltered, and I noticed he was only kissing my neck so he could look behind us. Squeezing my leg, he stopped. He saw something. Then his kisses returned, traveling to my ear.

Hot breath tickled me, as he declared, "We're leaving. Keep up, but don't rush."

The biker planned to follow someone. I obeyed his lead but then saw something that stopped me in my tracks. One small hesitation, and I tripped. My feet left the ground.

Levi caught me by the small of my back, setting me right almost instantly.

Damn. He had the reflexes of a cat. Without them, I'd have cracked my head open.

"Sorry, these heels," I said to explain and regroup.

Levi offered his arm.

Taking it, I limped on, slowing us down. It wasn't just my ankle, he trailed someone I recognized. The biker was in plain clothes, but I knew him from the Asphalt Gods MC club house. The face tattoo, a name scrawled over his eye so crudely you couldn't read it gave him away.

Another prospect was in the area. Why? Was he spying on me? Did he have the same mission? Killer hadn't said a thing about it.

The man Levi pursued mounted a motorcycle I more than recognized. I'd know it anywhere. The Harley-Davidson softail was mine.

What the actual fuck?

Levi started his hog, and it didn't take much for me to rush onto the back. I wanted to catch the fucker too.

We ended up downtown Nashville, in the heart of the city, down Broadway. Hordes of people were in the street. This part was closed to traffic, but our mark didn't care and neither did Levi. His motorcycle weaved through the people hopping from bar to bar. I'd lost the God we chased. But Levi steered us into the alley behind a honky-tonk.

We parked right beside my motorcycle. Fuck what was that fuckers name? He'd parked my bike there in the fucking dirty alley beside a dumpster. Orange and sleek it didn't exactly look like it belonged to a woman, but it did. I'd sunk my savings to buy it. I put the dents and scrapes in the metal learning to ride it.

Levi cut his engine. I leapt off his motorcycle, but he didn't move.

He explained, "Fireball runs with my enemy, the Asphalt Gods MC. We'll wait for him to come out here."

Fireball, yeah, that was it. If he was patched. Had he been? I'd been at Royal Road for months now but hadn't heard.

"You're enemy?" I played dumb.

Levi cracked his head sideways. "You've not heard about me?"

"Not really."

"You sure?"

I surrendered, "Everyone says you're a monster, but I don't believe it."

He smiled at that, offering me his hand. Placing my fingers into his palm, I let him yank me back on his hog. He wanted me in his lap. I obliged. Inching up my miniskirt, I straddled him.

"I figure we've got time before he comes back out," Levi said, with an arched eyebrow.

"Time for what?" I asked, knowingly.

His hands zipped right up my shirt. They were ice cold from the ride. The sensation wasn't exactly unwanted but had surprised me all the same. The biker undid my bra and had my tits out in the cool breeze before I knew it. At least he covered them with his warm mouth. His bald head dipped down further, and he sucked a nipple into his mouth. I smelted in the heat he caused to rise in me.

As monstrous as he looked, Levi was all softness with my breasts. Fuck. I wanted so much to take in every movement, to enjoy it but all I could think about was Fireball rushing out into the alley and giving me away.

"Why are they your enemy?" I asked him, ignoring the pleasure he caused.

He spoke to my chest. "Those Gods killed my sister, strung her up a telephone pole and left her for dead."

"Oh, fuck. I didn't know." Holy hell. I really hadn't known.

That sounded abysmal. Inexcusable. The Asphalt Gods I knew didn't seem capable of such atrocities, but I'd also learned since agreeing to prospect that all bikers kept their misdeeds under wraps for good reason.

"She was pregnant too. Probably one of theirs for all I know. Anyway, I'm going to do the same to this fucker after I question him of course. Too bad it's not one of their women." Levi spoke between ravaging my breasts.

"You'd do that to one of their women?" I breathed heavily.

"Yeah, that's all I want. To catch one of their women, torture her and make the evil fuckers feel my pain. Vengeance. They say you dig two graves, but I'm willing to die for it. That Eve bitch is one of them, you know. I wanted to string her up but Hallow stopped me. When I saw you with him, I couldn't stand it. I wasn't going to let him take you from me."

His kisses on my chest became savage.

"Take me from you?" Shit. Did he know about me?

"Killed me to see him with the woman I planned to fuck," he said, and I understood his meaning.

Levi's hand fell to my skirt and ran up my thigh, searching. I rose to allow it. He found my panties and tugged them forward, so he could get his fingers in me. Fingers, he went in with two right away. I groaned. His teeth grazed my nipple as he fucked me with his hand. Then he bit down as he went harder.

Holy smokes.

I grabbed the back of his bald head to hold on as he practically punched a hole in my pussy. His knuckles scraped my clit deliciously as he did. Writhing on his lap, I breathed rapidly as I bore the pleasure I hadn't had in so long. His face met mine, but he didn't go in to kiss my lips. A cocky look on his face, he watched me climax. He knew exactly what he was doing, getting me off. I came in no time.

The man removed his fingers.

I shuddered as our connection faded.

He went for his jeans. "Fuck Hallow. You're my bitch, and you're going to ride my hog," he said, unzipping himself.

Oh, fuck, how I wanted to, more than anything, but I had to get out of here before Fireball outed me. Levi would kill me instead.

"I don't think I can. I'm spent," I said, breathlessly.

Levi leaned into me again as he positioned his cock under me.

"You can come again. It'll be easier with your pussy relaxed," he said into the crook of my neck. "Easier to fit."

Levi took my hand to his massive dick. I couldn't get a hand around it. His head still in my way as he lingered, placing tender kisses on my neck, I couldn't even see it. But feeling it was enough. There was no way in hell. Besides, I had to get out of here.

"I think I'm going to be sick," I yelped, warning him.

I threw up over the side of the motorcycle. Partly, I did have a nervous stomach but vomiting on command was a skill I learned in the circus, trying my hand at magic. You could swallow about anything small and throw it up later.

Abracadabra, motherfucker.

"Too many margaritas," I explained, wiping my lips.

"Two?" Levi exclaimed, zipping his pants.

"I'm a lightweight." I pretended to be mortified as I tugged my shirt down, covering myself up. "Can you just take me home?" I produced tears.

Thinking about Levi finding out about me, it wasn't difficult. But I'd learned to cry on command as well.

Monster or not, Levi wasn't immune to a woman's tears.

"Alright. Fireball can wait," he said, his voice full of concern.

Bloody Hell, that only made me want him more as we rode off, heading back to Royal Road.

Still in character I ran off to my bedroom when we made it back. Levi didn't follow.

I texted Killer, "What the fuck is Fireball doing in Nashville?"

"Making sure you're doing your job," he answered.

"Got another spy at Royal Road?"

"Maybe."

"I need to know."

"Above your paygrade. But know we're set up to go when you give the order."

"What you want takes time," I texted. "Unless you don't want him to fall for me?"

"No. Take your time. You've got until Halloween."

"He said you murdered his sister?"

"We did. Is that a problem?"

"No. Just don't want to go in blind."

"The less you know the better. More believable that way."

I avoided Levi for the rest of the week because I really didn't know what to do anymore. The Asphalt Gods MC did murder his sister. No wonder he was itching to kill them all. I'd thought he was the murderer. Sending my club in to kill everyone at Royal Road didn't sit right with me anymore. Hell, it never really did, but I'd bit off more than I could chew, and I didn't know how to escape yet.

Once I worked up the courage to talk to Levi, he was altogether gone.

I asked Paisley what was going on.

"Goliaths out. Leviathan's our only Enforcer, guarding our king. Kingpin's about to go through some shit, I've heard."

Apparently, Levi had been checking out Shakey's for a reason. The shit hit the fan at Royal Road. I only saw him in the club when he was next to his master, Kingpin. I didn't dare approach him then. There was trouble in paradise, and their Prez was on a rampage. And Levi never found me when he could. Maybe I'd scared him off with my vomiting act. Killer kept texting asking how it was going, but I had no news. I lied and told him that things were going as planned. But I was having second thoughts about betraying everyone.

Then the unthinkable happened.

Sky, the President's Ol' Lady was nearly massacred. One of the whores and Prez's other ex, Junebug had sliced her up, almost killing her and her baby. The news had come as a shock. Though I had tried to keep my distance, I cried real tears hearing how she suffered. And it was all a little too close to what happened to Levi's sister in my opinion. I wondered if the Asphalt Gods MC had anything to do with it. I wanted to tell Levi of my worries, but he stayed with his Prez in the hospital day and night. So, I never saw him to know how he was holding up after witnessing such a thing.

While they were gone, things at Royal Road ran pretty much as usual. Pagan, left in charge of the show in his President's absence was an easy replacement. Loyal to his boss, he didn't steer from his wishes. But the whole club felt his loss and his pain. One of theirs had been taken from the property and mutilated in a bloodcurdling way. They all felt partly responsible. Afterall, they were supposed to protect Kingpin and what was his at all costs.

One night, Opry approached me. He had a plan that might cheer up everyone once his President returned. He needed my help to pull it off. I happily agreed. But the next night proved, he also wanted something else from me. He caught me just as I entered the dressing room. My top was still off. The biker sat at my dressing table with his dick out. Hard, it looked as thin and tall as him. He rose to his feet and made his way over. Holding it, he wagged his dick at me.

"Figured we'd be spending a lot of time together. We might as well have some fun doing it."

"I can't," I pushed him away. "I belong to Leviathan."

CHAPTER 7

Maren

Stepping on the stage, I spotted the biker covered in black tentacles. Leviathan sat up front on one of the couches. Other than being a casino, this place was a basic strip club. Girls gave lap dances on those divans right in front of everyone. The voyeurism, the purpose, because some of our important guests just liked to watch.

I hadn't seen him for over a month now. I couldn't help the smile from growing on my face when I spied him. Yeah, I'd heard him and Kingpin were back from the hospital, finally. Sky had survived and she was still pregnant with twins. Something else the women chattered about.

Leaning back, the monstrous man spread his arms and legs wide, engulfing the sofa. My heart fluttered seeing him again. I trembled as I began my act.

His sultry eyes didn't leave me during my show. When I swung my booty and bounced up and down, I twerked a bit. Something new, a nod to the strippers, before I weaved into a difficult posture. Withdrawing my bikini top, I thought of Levi. It was all for him. I gave my routine a little bit more than

I ever did. More sensuality. More passion. Everyone hollered for more as they always did, but I only worried about him.

Unlike the other dancers, I would not remove my bottoms. However, for Levi alone, I did take the time to touch myself more than I would normally. Calling attention to the best parts of my body, I took more time than usual too. I had a grown woman's body, with plenty of tits, hips, and ass. A softness to my navel that made my belly dance more enticing.

Levi's mouth hung open, like he appreciated every movement.

All the men loved it when I spread my legs, bent backwards, grabbed my ankles from behind and looked through my legs. My pelvis hanging above my head, I dropped to the stage. I couldn't imagine if I'd been naked, stretched out like that. My pussy on full display. Or maybe I could. My eyes locked onto Levi's sultry gaze. He wasn't looking at my eyes. His stare settled on the strip of fabric hiding my pussy in this awkward pose. His features dripped with an intense sexual energy. Therefore, when I ended my show, I was flustered. I didn't rush to the dressing room like I usually did. I crawled off the stage toward him, like he was my prey.

The monster invited me onto his lap much like the last time I saw him. It'd been too long.

Tonight, nothing was stopping me. Holding my breasts to cover them in one arm, I took his hand and lowered myself on him. Blushing, I was so happy to see him. I'd really thought he'd been turned off by the way we parted before.

The biker smirked. Taking my arm, he moved it away completely. My breasts bounced free. On stage was one thing, being topless was something I'd gotten used to while dancing at the Asphalt Gods' clubhouse. However, I was never truly a stripper. I'd never given a lap dance, let alone with a crowd around me.

Levi's eyes plunged to my naked tits. My chest heaved thinking of how tenderly he'd kissed them before and how ferociously. He licked his lips like he wanted to taste them again.

But I could feel a million eyes on us. I had to keep calm. I tried my best to focus solely on him but was failing.

"Hi, you're back," I said awkwardly to break the ice.

"I am," he said simply, but his eyes tunneled into me.

His intense gaze scared me. Then I realized there was no dancing, I sat right on the mountain in his pants. I raised up, pulling myself away from him to start moving. Levi held the wrist he grabbed to free my breasts. He wrenched it behind my back. His other hand came up and snatched a breast a bit too hard.

Leaning in he whispered against my neck, "Who are you?"

I didn't understand. We'd been over this. I thought we were past it. "What do you mean?"

"You told Opry you were mine."

Oh, I had.

"But you're not a stripper. You don't know how to give a lap dance."

"No, I told you I'm not." Didn't I?

"You're not who you say. Maybe you were. But you're a different person now."

My word. Was he on to me?

His breath tickled my ear. "What did you think that I never caught Fireball? I know you're a spy."

I was in trouble now. He actually knew.

"How long have you known?" I said, inaudibly.

"It doesn't matter. You're lucky I've been busy. Everyone will know if you don't act like you want to ride this dick. Move your ass. Give them a show to remember you by."

The danger of it all made me forget everyone was looking at us. He let go of my breast and wound his hand down to catch my hip. His hand guided me for a moment, rocking me over his pelvis. Even so, he never let go of my arm that he twisted behind my back. He'd captured me. I couldn't get away from him if I wanted to. My body aching for him, I didn't want to get away, all but for the people staring at us.

My eyes hooded, I moved on my own, teasing his package. Rocking my ass slowly over the mound in his jeans so everyone could see, I got lost in the moment. Levi grabbed that thin strip of fabric between me and him, rubbing his knuckles against my wet pussy like he had in the alley. With my restrained arm, he hauled my body into him. My tits smashed against his chin, almost engulfing his face. He stuck out his tongue and licked my nipple. I ground myself hard against his hand, craving him inside me, all over me.

He growled, "I've got something else for you to ride."

"Not here," I pipped.

"But you claimed to be mine. And I don't do that. Ever. Do you want everyone to know about you? Do you want me to tell my Prez?"

I said nothing. Fuck. He knew I was a spy. This was when I was supposed to hit the speed dial and call Killer on speaker. But my phone was in the dressing room.

Levi hissed in my ear, "I'm going to undo my pants and you're going to sit down really nice. You're going to take my big dick like a champ right in front of my brothers. Holler my name and say your pussy is mine. Or I'll let them all know you're a spy for the Asphalt Gods MC. You'll be dead in less than one minute flat."

Leviathan unfastened his pants and positioned his large cock beneath me on the cusp of my sex, right in front of everyone. The fleshy head of his dick waited between my folds. The sensation drove me mad with desire. Twisting my head for a moment, I observed the people watching, the members, the bikers, the whores, Paisley, Cccc, and Eve. Plus, the multitude of people I didn't know. Men in suits and ladies who looked like they stepped off the runway. They couldn't see Levi's dick, only me spread out on his lap, topless and gasping. I was just another whore around here, but I felt more than exposed.

The music finally changed. Memphis and the others graced the stage. The crowd shifted their attention.

Leviathan reached up and snatched the crown off my head, taking my platinum hair down. Grabbing a handful, he threatened me more, not knowing it only aroused me. Still, this was too much for me. I craved danger, not humiliation. I'd never done it in public before. And although, I planned to do anything I could to get close to this biker, even have sex with him. It was something I thought I could work up the courage to do in private.

Leviathan moved under me, brushing his dick against my clit but didn't surge my body down on him.

He was giving me the choice, sort of.

"Fuck you and you'll let me live?" I clarified.

"That was your plan anyhow. What were you going to do once you were caught?"

"It's complicated," I said, because I couldn't say I planned to call in the Asphalt Gods and have them slaughter everyone. That would get me killed for sure. Hopefully, he didn't know that.

"You can tell me after you fuck me. Right here right now. Show me what you're willing to do for those maniacs." He tugged my hair back harder, exposing my neck. His mouth landed on the base of it. I lowered a little and that was all it took.

His hand shifted from my hair to my ass cheek heaving my body down as he thrusted up. His dick entered me but not much more than the tip.

Fuck a duck.

It packed a punch. I'd tensed up. His cock really must be colossal.

Levi murmured in my ear, "How are you a whore for the Gods if you can't even take this dick?"

"I'm not a whore. I'm probate," I admitted, quietly.

Levi propelled me down further. I gulped at the pain as he stretched me.

"You've not taken on a bunch of Gods then?"

"No, not even one." My forehead touched his. "I'm earning my patch."

He forced further inside, stretching my pussy wider. I yelped, calling attention to us and instantly reddened.

Levi didn't care. But he was quiet, but his face screamed he was so angry with me. No one here would think anything was amiss though. They'd think he was merely mad at me for flirting with someone or something. "Why should I believe you?" He asked, aloud.

"You can't," I answered, honestly. "But it's the truth."

Frustrated, Levi yanked his dick out of me and zipped his pants. Before I could bolt, he snatched me and dragged me through the casino by the hair of my head.

"Where are you taking me?"

"To the basement, where we used to take our prisoners."

CHAPTER 8

Maren

Before I knew it, I was locked in a room with the monster. With all the whips and chains on the wall, I could only assume we were in a sex dungeon.

Hugging my bare breasts, I sat on the edge of the big bed, almost the only furniture in the room.

Looming over me, Levi questioned me. He shot out one after another. I couldn't keep up.

When I didn't answer anything, he warned, "We can do this the easy way or the hard way."

"What, fuck?" The biker's dick had just been inside me, even if only a bit. As much as I was petrified, I yearned for it to return.

"No. I wanted you to tell me about Killer's plans, but you're right. You didn't actually fuck me out there. Why should I let you live?"

Staring up at him, I sucked my lips in. Holding out empty hands, I raised my shoulders. I didn't have an answer. Leviathan was even hotter when he was mad. Flushing and fuming, he looked like he could kill me. His muscles twitched and flexed. His hands opened and closed as he fought the urge. When he yanked a pistol out of nowhere, I creamed my panties.

"I'll just take what I want right now," he growled.

"Or what?" I squeaked.

Automatically, I felt for my phone. This was it. The monster was going to kill me.

Levi pulled my phone out of his pocket. "Looking for this?" He held it up to my face.

I hadn't even been restrained, and he unlocked it easily.

"Stupid to use a face ID," he ridiculed me. "Fucking amateur."

I sat up on my knees, but what could I do? Attack him? Maybe if he didn't have a gun.

He scrolled through it. "You've deleted everything."

"Always. I'm not so dumb."

He tucked it back into his pants. "That's okay. We've got a tech guy who can look at it tomorrow."

Fuck. He'd know everything.

"I'll have my answers. But until then, you'll pay up."

Leviathan descended on my body, knocking me back. His gun rammed against my side, between my ribs. His hand wrapped around my throat. The weight of him surged his package to the right spot. A raging hard on whacked my pussy.

"Why even fuck me?" I questioned him. I'd thought this man would go straight to killing.

"Can't kill you yet. Might have questions about what I find on your phone."

"Surprised you'd want anything to do with an Asphalt God."

"You've been teasing me since you got to Royal Road. Making me want you. You planned to, didn't you? You planned to fuck me to earn your patch. Then betray me."

"Yes," I breathed out, easily. He wasn't strangling me. Not yet.

"How long did you plan to keep up your ruse?"

"Until you fell in love with me."

"Impossible. I never would have."

"Until you tried to kill me."

"That's possible." Levi called attention to how he still threatened my life. "All I'd have to do is squeeze, either one. I could crush your windpipe or blow a hole in you."

I sucked in a breath. "Killer said you were a monster. Everyone says it."

"I'll show you a monster."

My mouth fell open as I breathed fast.

His eyes got all squinty. "This only turns you on?"

Turning my chin, I was afraid to admit it.

77

"You've got a death wish!" he exclaimed like he'd found me out.

"I wouldn't say that."

"You do if you're messing with the likes of me."

I couldn't disagree there.

Levi removed his hand from my throat. I coughed. He'd gotten off me, but kept his gun trained on my head.

His grip sank as he pointed it lower. "Take that off." He spoke of my bottoms which were like a skirt and underwear combined.

Hooking my thumbs in the sides, I slipped them down slowly as if it was all part of my performance. Rolling my neck, I danced them off like it was part of my seductive show. When it reached my ankles, I kicked it away with a flare.

Closing his eyes, Levi shook his head. I was getting to him.

"Lay back and spread your legs."

I leaned back on my elbows and opened my thighs wide. My pussy was as smooth as can be. I couldn't risk a hair to show during my act.

"Touch yourself. Your tits, your pussy."

Was this what he was into? Earlier he'd wanted everyone to watch us and now he wanted to watch me play with myself.

Up on one elbow, I ran my hand over my chest, taking the time to tweak my nipples. I rolled the tips between my fingers, responding to my touch but also to memories of him. Then I moved that same hand down, running my palm across my navel to my smooth lips. Slipping my fingers between my moist folds, I tickled my own clit. Letting myself genuinely enjoy it, my head fell back. I arched my back thinking of the night with Levi in the alley when we almost fucked. Closing my legs on my hand, I let out all too real moan.

Levi kept his gun on me. "Open those thighs. Show me your pussy."

I obeyed him and spread them as far as I could. It was really far. I watched Levi's eyes grow as big as saucers.

"Suck on your fingers."

Okay, that was odd, but I complied. Did it as sexy as I could. I imagined his dick in my mouth.

"Now, fuck yourself. Get ready for me."

I started with one finger.

"I'm much larger than that."

Levi didn't drop his weapon as he slipped down his pants, revealing his massive Mac Truck.

Judas Priest.

While my eyes studied the size of him, he'd gotten some lube from somewhere. He greased his column, preparing to force feed me a large pizza. The thing couldn't be sixteen inches, but Paisley was right. Saying a foot wouldn't do it justice because of the girth alone. I forgot all the whore's scales and came up with one of my own. The damned thing was a monster like the man himself. The size of it alone was fucking, well, monstrous. That was the word. The biker could kill someone with that monster of a dick. Literally, choke them or hit them over the head with it. Fuck, his dick would rise from the dead and kill on its own.

Putting three fingers together, I dug them into myself. It'd never prepare me.

I didn't know if I could ever get ready for the likes of his monster. But the peril the whole situation proposed did things to me I couldn't explain. I felt like I was flying high again on the trapeze. The rush sent tingles all over as Levi tackled me. His massive body covered me.

His fingers replaced my own. "You're pretty tight. But I'm not stopping until you can take the whole thing."

"I don't think I can," I said, honestly.

"Could take all night, but you will."

"You going to wrap it?"

"Condoms are too small. They break anyway.

"I'm hoping you're clean?"

"That's odd to ask when a man's got a gun pointed at you."

I could feel it back at my ribcage.

"But yeah. I am. I'm clean. I hope you're on the pill. I don't want more kids."

"Of course. I don't want any more either," I said, before I caught my mistake. That was something I didn't want him to know.

Levi rose up and cocked the gun. For a minute I thought he was going to shoot me and end it all right then. But he stood and laid it on the table behind him.

"Aren't you worried, I'll snatch that gun and end you?"

"No. I'm not taking any chances."

Levi went for the chains that hung on the wall. "Sit up," he commanded.

He wrapped them tightly around my arms and torso like his tentacle tattoos were real and squeezing me to death. Though he left my breasts unbound on purpose, he let the end of it wrap gently around my neck, like it was just for looks.

Standing back, he stroked himself a few times, admiring his work. Only my bottom half was free. I wouldn't be doing any more dancing.

"Just try and get away now."

I had no words. I'd never been so turned on in my life.

He joined me on the bed on his knees and knocked me over with one finger.

"You couldn't take my dick in the club, but you will now."

Taking the lower half of me, he pulled my ass up as he entered me. Well, like before, he barely got inside.

Levi all but growled out. He liked the struggle. "Too tight to be a whore, but still a whore."

The damn monstrous dick just wouldn't slide up there easily.

"I told you that I was trying to earn my patch. Can't earn it by fucking your way to the top."

Levi thrusted forward again, making me pant as he strained my pussy to the max.

"How can you fuck anyone with this huge thing?" I complained.

"Plenty of women here can take all of my dick."

"You've been with all of them. They probably enjoy getting fisted too."

"Almost all the whores here. And yes, a few of them like to be fisted, too. Who was the last man you fucked? Hallow?"

"No. No one since I left the circus."

"Someone special?"

Frack. Flattening my lips, I didn't answer that.

"Yet, you're willing to fuck me for a patch. Fuck me over, too."

Levi grew angrier by the second as he battled to work his dick inside me. My body reacted. Overstimulated, I wanted him inside me more than anything. I knew I should calm down so I could accommodate his size, but the risk of fighting him was too tempting. I only tightened up.

Levi groaned in my ear. "Why fight me? Your pussy's already tight enough. This is what you wanted. Sex with this monster."

Pulling back, his dick still inside me a hair, his hands took the underside of my knees. He drove them up much farther than someone's hips would normally allow, contorting me against my will. Levi was using my flexibility against me, splaying me wide. Not only was I chained, but I was also bent in a more obliging position.

"There. I'm sure that will give me the leverage I need. You're so wet already. I know you can take this dick. Relax, Maren. Or this is going to hurt you even more than I want it to. Maybe in the alley I would've but after finding out about you, I don't plan to hold back. You're going to get exactly what you've been working for."

Then it really began, him fucking me. He put his Mac Truck into overdrive.

I heaved a breath, in and out, as he punched himself inside me, outspreading my pussy, painfully so. He didn't hold back. Levi panted above me, a slight smile on his face. He relished forcing his dick into my slick vice. The chains between us cut into my body with him against them. Still, I let go and tried to enjoy the ride. I fought the urge to expel him from my body as his fat dick felt too substantial to be entering me. My insides twisted feeling somewhat sick, but it never erased my yearning.

He was just too large, but he was inside me, filling me. Then the man complained that I could take some more.

More?

He hadn't been all the way in. Snarling, he pressed his pedal to the metal and jolted all the way up me. It'd been like pulling off a Band-Aid, agonizing yet fucking rewarding. Owning me, he violated me with every flick of his hips. Splitting my body in two with each thrust, Levi's monstrous dick wrecked my pussy.

The discomfort mutated into unknown pleasure, but it never became easier for him to really move. It was worse at first then so much better. Tension built between stinging blows. I was almost down for the count. One. Two. Three. I came when Levi did. He jolted over me and pumped slowly, enjoying himself.

I noticed he didn't pull out in time.

Motherfucker.

Then the man kissed my forehead, my cheek as I tried to catch my breath. A rush of chilly air hit me when he left the bed. He left the room, locking the door behind him. Locking me in. He completely disappeared and left me chained up on the bed.

CHAPTER 9

Leviathan

"Going to ask Cece's new nurse to the Halloween Orgy," Riff said to the lot of us as we waited for Church to begin.

I didn't give a flying fuck.

Drumming my fingers, I waited for our sermon. We weren't in a church waiting on the preacher. No, we were in the Throne Room with its soundproof walls and bolted doors, the conference room at Royal Road. That was the name for the clubhouse of the Royal Bastards MC in Nashville which doubled as our entertainment venue. Settled in the industrial area outside Nashville, the group of three large warehouses hosted our legitimate and illegal business, not to mention our fun. We waited on the king around here, the President of this motorcycle club to come and get caught up himself.

Kingpin had been away staying by the bedside of his Ol' Lady in the hospital. I knew because I'd been there as well, day and night, guarding him, being his only Enforcer now. He was an important man with many enemies. I was scarier than him but not as scary as the man he'd just fired from the job. It was true, I'd already been his Enforcer for years but only a backup. Therefore, I'd been allowed to do my own thing for a while now around the club. I had been an officer enjoying the

Morgan Jane Mitchell

benefits without doing much work, with even less supervision, even being loaned out to other chapters of this club like a Nomad. All because Kingpin felt he owed me.

He did.

He wouldn't let me enact my rightful revenge on a rival club. As it was now, I was stuck at my Prez's beck and call. Luckily, he was spending all his time in the Big House. Not jail, though he'd been there before, and you'd never hear the end of it. That's what he called the third large warehouse he'd made into his residence. He'd been holed up in the Big House with his Ol' Lady who'd just been released from the hospital. Wouldn't let anyone else do a thing for her. He didn't trust anyone.

Couldn't blame him after what happened to her.

His new wife recovered from some serious and grotesque injuries she endured at the hands of one of our sweetbutts. We kept all kinds of women at Royal Road, and they were the whores for anyone's use. We used these women hard, and they loved it. They were well kept women, fed and clothed by us, given jobs, and protected by us bikers. I knew them all well. Ever since Chloe my wife did me dirty, I'd been having all the fun I could handle with the club whores. For one thing, I planned to never fall in love again. Hell, I had years of fun after Chloe admitted what she did to me. So, I knew Junebug well. She'd been one fantastic lay.

That crazy bitch had been one of our Prez's favorites so when she chose you, you wanted a taste of what he was having. She was a top shelf whore. And you couldn't really say no to her. Woman basically worked as his bodyguard too, on a much more personal level before his new girl, Sky showed up. Therefore, Junebug had been a goddamn boss around here along with her bookend, her cousin Memphis. Kingpin's other ex he seemed to have forgotten about.

If I were him, I wouldn't take my eye off Memphis. She was just as irrational. Just as senseless. Maybe more so. Since I was responsible for him, that whore was my problem.

Kingpin finally dipped his nib into a much younger woman and ended up marrying her ass. He kicked Junebug to the curb along with his main Enforcer Goliath. Come to find out they had been in love all these years, but Prez thought they were fixing to defect to the mob. Couldn't blame him for thinking it, either. An Enforcer couldn't go keeping secrets like I was about to. They'd end up dead.

It was a risk I was willing to take.

After Kingpin kicked his whore out of this club, Junebug decided to inflict her pain on his new woman and therefore him. Bitch cut the man's initials into the poor girl, all over her but carefully enough not to kill her or her unborn child. A fitting punishment in Junebug's insane head since Kingpin liked to mark his women that way with a simple K crudely etched into them. It wasn't reserved for the special ones either. Just someone he wanted to play with. The man had never gotten a woman tatted like we members did.

Man was smart.

I wished my wife Chloe would have hers removed. The only reason Chloe wasn't my ex-wife was because she wouldn't sign the papers. And my little girl Haven was the only reason Chloe still lived at the Eagle's Nest, our place away from the dangers of the clubhouse, where our families lived. Not that I didn't think of the other two kids as my daughters still. It would take more than a few years of truth to erase my love for those girls. Consequently, I worried about what would happen to the three of them after I defied my President.

Pagan, our Vice-President ran the show while Kingpin was away but wouldn't stray from our President's wishes like I hoped he would.

Regardless, I'd made my plans. I'd keep them to myself this time.

He reminded the men. "Let's keep the dumbfuckery to a minimum today. Prez is back. Riff, Halloween's a whole two weeks away. The last nurse you were boning is barely cold."

After witnessing Kingpin empty a clip into that nurse over what she helped Junebug do to his woman, I'd have my vengeance on the club who killed my sister with or without his permission.

"Have you seen Mary?" Riff went on.

With his long hair and leather, Riff was a discount version of our President. He wanted to be him, title, and all, but didn't hold a candle to the man himself. Brother felt entitled to his position because he came from a family of outlaw bikers.

"Yeah, we have eyes. But she doesn't look like she'd go to an orgy, Riff," Villain said, in his usual sarcastic tone.

He spit out shells because he was always chewing on something. Pistachios today. Power hungry prick was our young, asshole Sergeant at Arms who looked like a Disney prince, complete with swept back blond hair. With three daughters, I knew that all too well.

Pagan added, "I was careful to do a background check this time. I can guarantee you, this nurse doesn't even celebrate Halloween. She escaped from some Amish village or something, some cult. Girl's probably a virgin."

One of my brothers who I felt was a brother, Pagan endured the same curse as me. People feared him for his barbaric looks and his position. Sometimes for good reason, sometimes not. We had to stay frightening, but it made getting close to anyone a problem. Not only that, our positions in the club also made it problematic.

His sister was blind, and this had to be the sixth nurse he'd hired to take care of her at the clubhouse. He'd been fucking most of them, but not getting too close. Until Jassica. And that bitch ran off. Not before she burned down half the place.

Fucking Cece's nurses seemed to be Riff's thing now though.

But like I said, I didn't give a fuck.

"Well, even better. This year, Mary's going to celebrate Halloween. Dress up and all. She's gonna be a goblin. Goblin this dick," Riff belted out.

The other members crowded in the room laughed on cue. There had to be more than fifty men here, but only the officers sat at the table. The room grew louder and smokier by the second.

Thankfully, Kingpin busted through the door in the next instance and shut Riff up.

A respectful silence fell as Kingpin slammed the heavy door shut.

Gone was his signature long hair, but the rest of him was very much the same. The biker had to outdo us all. He had to be the most biker out of everyone, in looks at least. Where most of us only wore our cuts over our t-shirts, maybe some shit kickers, he was always in black leather from head to toe. Some of us wore flannels and jeans like I wore today since it was colder than a witch's tit out suddenly.

But not him, our President came shirtless, showing off his piercings and tattoos under the cut he wore. The sun-bleached vest had been handed down from the President before him, tattered and worn. In leather pants that had goddamn leather fringe going down the legs, he stomped in like he owned the place. And he did. Biker had about as many tattoos as me. However, where he had gothic crows, crosses, and devilish imagery, I had a sea monster's tentacles going up my sides and on my bald head. But yeah, I wore a toboggan, too. I was fucking freezing.

Motherfucker dubbed me Leviathan on account of the tats and my real name, Levi. It wouldn't be the name I chose, but we didn't choose them.

Some of us wore a chain or two, a couple of badass rings on our fingers. I had a couple myself. However, there wasn't a speck of Kingpin not touched with jewelry of spikes, chains, skulls, dangling earrings even. Prez wore eyeliner and black nail polish just to distinguish himself from all of us country bikers in Nashville. Like Opry and Thorn who liked cowboy hats and boots with their motorcycle vests.

You'd think with all he had going on, Kingpin might appear gay, but no, man looked like he stepped out of a heavy metal video and would eat you, like drink your blood, scary shit. And they called me a monster. Kingpin pulled all this shit off, presenting as alpha AF. If any of us did half the crazy shit he did, we'd be laughed out of the club.

Besides, he was king around here and did what he pleased. He created Royal Road twenty years ago right before he became President of the Nashville Chapter of the Royal Bastards MC. He grew the club into the empire it was in Music City today. And the multitude of guests Royal Road brought in, gambling on anything and everything supported us all.

I was living the dream.

Fuck, I was going to miss it.

Only one closer look at our Prez told me he wasn't all the same. Guilt weighed heavily on our mad King, sobering him.

That wasn't a good look on him.

Pagan opened the proceedings, handing the gavel back to him.

"How's she holding up," he asked our Prez.

Kingpin lit a cigarette and took his seat, a literal ornate throne upholstered in red velvet. Slumping back, he put his boot on his knee.

After taking a long draw, he blew out smoke and spoke at the same time. "Brothers, my Ol' Lady is a fighter. She's survived what would kill any of us men and continues to love me. I'm one lucky son of a bitch. The next member to betray me better remember Junebug and Goliath. I loved them both, dearly, but if you fuck with me, prepare to die like they did."

We all knew Kingpin didn't kill either of them himself. Goliath took his own life. He only died because he was fiercely in love with Junebug and wanted to kill Kingpin because she'd been slain on his orders and rightfully so. The fucker was that loyal to our Prez. Loyal enough to take his own life rather than kill his master.

I wasn't that loyal.

But I did get the meaning behind my President's words. And when I took revenge for my sister's death on the Gods without his blessing, I could only hope he understood.

I couldn't say I didn't miss Goliath. Gross motherfucker had been my roommate, a nasty one at that, but he'd grown on me. I'd been staying with my brother, Horror when his roomie Payday spent his nights hooked up with some woman in the city. And Horror was mostly staying at his house over in the Eagle's Nest, where most of the old ladies stayed. He had Tonya set up over there. I'd taken the first chance to escape Goliath's mess, but I hadn't known about Junebug staying there with him while I was gone.

And with him gone for good, I still didn't have the place to myself. Kingpin gave Goliath's house out from under me to our live-in star, Eve. I roomed with Opry now, officially, but still went to Horror's empty place when I had a woman over.

Prez kept it short and sweet as he usually did, and I realized I missed him at the helm too. Much better than the long-drawn-out bullshit Pagan put us through. Thankfully, I hadn't been around for much of it. I'd been in the hospital guarding Prez. He closed Church with the bang of his gavel.

The men picked up their conversation right where they left off.

"Riff, I tell you what, I'm Southern Freewill Baptism, but I'd take one of them cult girls any day," Horror said.

"What about Tonya?"

"Tonya's going to be performing on Halloween as a witch. Since Eve's a no show. But she thinks she is one. For real. Into crystals and shit. But she's a good cook."

"Good cook, my ass. What you eatin tonight, Horror?" Villain asked.

"Pussy pot pie, mind your business."

Kingpin had been headed toward the exit, but he stopped by at the mention of Eve's name.

"Opry, why isn't Eve performing on Halloween?"

"Says she's sick. Actually, she said she feels lower than a snake's belly," Opry mocked her southernisms.

We were all southern around here, Eve was just extra.

"It's two weeks away?" Kingpin stated the obvious, clearly upset.

Opry said, "Girl won't go on. Been sick all month. You ask her."

Without a response, our Prez left the building.

Pagan waited for everyone to clear out of the Throne Room. He told them, "Brothers, don't know why any of you have dates. It's going to be raining titties on Halloween."

"How 'bout you, Leviathan? We didn't hear anything about revenge tonight," Riff mocked me.

"Prez has been through enough without my demands," I lied to keep him off my trail.

Riff told all the officers, "Boys, Levi's preoccupied with other matters. Maren's hotter than a two-dollar pistol. We saw you two last night. You staked your claim to her, alright."

They didn't know the half of it. I couldn't wait to get to her. I'd left Maren chained up but just overnight. It was barely afternoon. She'd be okay, but she'd be fit to be tied. Bitch might be a spy for my enemies, but I sure did enjoy her pussy. And she was part of my plan. Bull had downloaded most of her messages from the cloud. I knew everything the Gods had planned and how to use her to get my revenge.

"Fuckers better stop harping on about the Halloween party. Maren's been helping me plan it all month," Opry said.

"What are you on about?" I asked him.

"Tonya's not performing. No offense, Horror, but she sucks."

"Sucks this dick," Horror tried to give Riff a run for his money. He fell flat.

Opry ignored them. "Of course, you've been cooped up in a hospital hallway, day and night and haven't heard. It's a surprise for our Prez. No, Eve won't perform for some reason. Says her stage fright is back too. I didn't want to tell Kingpin that. Anyway, once I figured she wouldn't change her mind, plans changed. Maren's helping me plan a special Halloween party for Prez. Going to bring the house down."

I bet she'd want to bring the house down.

"Our Halloween parties already rock," I said, not understanding.

"We're planning a haunted carnival. My idea was inspired by your girl. Since Maren's from the circus, she's been helping me procure the rides and freaks and shit. We're getting a black and orange tent and Ferris wheel."

"No biker gives a goddamn about a Ferris wheel." Our Halloween parties were very adult themed and famed in the area. Opry had gone mad.

"Listen, the rides are for the kids."

"Kids?"

"Yeah, your daughters are going to be there. Already talked to Chloe. We're opening it up to our families and the public. Bubba's performing."

"Bubba?" The Prez hated his brother with a passion.

"But don't worry, that's only until sunset. After dark anyone under eighteen will have to vacate the premises. We'll break to make sure. Sweetbutts will have to change anyhow. The carnival will remind you of all our other Halloween parties, only better. And we'll still host our orgy in here at midnight. If anyone still wants to partake since so many of you are pussy whipped now."

"And Maren is helping you?"

"Yeah, she has the know-how. She used to run one of those traveling shows."

"You think Kingpin will like this?"

"Hell, yeah. Our haunted carnival's going to bring in a lot of dough. We might be able to finish rebuilding the arena in time for the spring."

When I got to the basement, Maren was gone, but the chains remained.

CHAPTER 10

Levi

I found her upstairs in Royal Road sitting with Opry at one of the tables, a map spread out between them. Dressed and looking well rested, she left the basement way earlier by the looks of her. Her hair was damn perfect. Did she have her nails done differently?

Taking her by the arm, I carted her up from her seat.

She yelped.

Opry complained.

"I just need a minute," I said to him, tearing her away to the corner to talk.

"Who let you go? Are you working with someone?"

"I let myself go. What? You don't think I can get out of some cheap chains? I'm a goddamn contortionist."

"You said you ain't that good."

Her eyes rolled back. "Newsflash, I lied."

Noticing Opry's glare, I walked her outside, out to the edge of the tree line so no one could overhear us. To them we would look like two lovers arguing.

"What else have you lied about?" I asked, even though I'd read her texts to Killer, the leader of my enemies. "And where have you been?"

"Been in the city this morning with the other girls, having a spa day." Maren wiggled her fingers, showing off her new black nails. "I'm not sure they'll last till Halloween."

Shit. She even left the property. Smelled like a million bucks, too. Bitch was fucking gorgeous as always, made what I planned to do to her all the harder.

"I can out you right now," I informed her. "You'll look pretty in your casket."

"But you said you wouldn't if I fucked you. I took that big dick of yours. You're welcome."

"Barely. I notice you can walk today. Maybe you are a whore."

"Fuck you. Paisley slipped me a pain pill. I woke up sore as all get out because of your mutant dick."

"Could've been worse. I could've killed you like you deserve."

Maren crossed her arms. "You said you'd let me live."

"That's before I read your texts."

Fear crept up, taking over her smug look. Her chest heaved, moving her arms. I could only think of her amazing tits.

"You know our plans?"

"Killer wanted you to make me fall in love with you?" I asked, my confusion clear in my voice.

"Yeah."

"Nice job," I said, laughing.

"I didn't have time. You were off babysitting that basket case of a President."

"Why wait until afterwards to tell me you're a spy? Why was that part of his plans?"

"I don't fucking know. To hurt you the most, I guess. I'm only a prospect. Do you think a man like Killer is taking my advice? I'm nothing to him."

"He told you I would kill you. And you were willing to do that? Die?"

She snorted. "Hell no. My plan always was to escape your wrath somehow."

Her naivety infuriated me. Seizing her arms, I took a hold of her. "How the fuck do you think you would escape me if I wanted to kill you?"

"I escaped last night. Didn't I?"

"I won't make that mistake again. You're not leaving my sight."

"What are you gonna do about that when you're guarding your President?"

"He's shacked up with his Ol' Lady now. He ain't leaving her anytime soon. The girl is still healing up. I've got all the time in the world to keep an eye on you. Now back to Killer and his plan. I already know, but I wanna hear more. Your life depends on it."

"Just kill me now," she said, testing me.

"I won't. I won't kill you. I'll just tell my brothers about a spy, and you'll have fifty men wanting a piece of you. I doubt they'd kill you right away. But if you liked last night, maybe that's what you want, to be raped and tortured out in our barn. You'd rather be dead."

Maren scowled, pouted but looked a bit excited. Fuck. She was nuttier than squirrel shit. But maybe not. Thankfully, she gave me what I wanted.

"I told you I don't know much, but from what I understand, Killer needs an excuse to slaughter everybody in this club. He's looking for the right to do it. His boss demands it."

"You're talking about Scar, that young pussy."

He sounded just like our Prez, looking for a justification. A way to enact his vengeance without getting his hands too dirty. They wanted no retaliation. Fucking pussies.

"I reckon. The President of their Mother Chapter has his own rules, and all the Chapters of the Asphalt Gods MC are bound by them. They run a tight ship."

Goddamn, I'm glad no one micromanaged us but Kingpin.

"They didn't used to run a tight anything," I said. "When they killed my sister, the General was in charge of Killer and let him run wild."

"Yeah, Killer doesn't want to start a war only because his new superior doesn't want one. He's thirsting for revenge. But Scar would replace him in a heartbeat."

"Revenge for what?"

"Y'all running him out of Tennessee. Humiliating him."

"He killed my sister all because one of his men impregnated my wife, twice, and once I found out I beat him to a bloody pulp. Running his club out of the state was fucking mercy."

"Just so you know, I didn't know any of this when I took the job. Nothing about your sister. Or your wife."

"Went in blind, did you? Agreed to kill a whole mess of innocent strangers for nothing. And they call me a monster."

"I was told you would murder anyone who claimed to be associated with my motorcycle club. You admitted as much. How are you any better than me or Killer?"

"You think I'd kill someone I fell in love with?"

"By all accounts you would. You said so yourself, you'd kill one of their women to hurt them. You wanted to kill Eve."

"Well, it's a good thing I didn't fall in love with you."

"I'm not even one of their women. I'm one of them, a prospect. A patched member if I had succeeded. An Asphalt God in my own right. I don't belong to any man in their club. They have their whores but also a place for women who ride and can fight."

"We have them too. Our Ol' Ladies."

"Your Ol' Ladies? Just like your Ol' Lady. She was out banging the rival club for a reason. Maybe she wanted a man who was faithful."

"No, she was just another whore. Just like most of the women around here. Just like you."

"Well, I'm not a whore, I'm a biker."

"You're still Killer's whore."

"I'm probate which means I will do anything for my club to earn my patch. Just like any man. Just like you did. You're Kingpin's whore."

I sure as hell wasn't. Not anymore. "Since when can you ride or fight?"

"You don't know anything about…"

"Spooky, is it? Why that road name?"

She blew out of her nose like a bull. "It's a long story. Let's just say I have demons that push me past my limits."

"Why should I let you live?" I asked her, but I was really asking myself.

"That's up to you."

Part of me wanted to kill her. But she wouldn't matter much to Killer and his club. But yeah, she'd be an excuse for them to wipe us out. Just like Eve would've been. It bothered me to no end that Kingpin had been right about leaving her alone.

Maren perplexed me. She hadn't had a hand in my sister's murder, and she had no idea what those men were capable of. However, ignorance wasn't a defense. She came to Royal Road planning to kill this whole damn club.

"Why are you even still here?" I asked.

She had the chance this morning getting her nails done to disappear. Was she still loyal to the Gods?

"Do you think I can return to Arkansas without completing my mission? Fireball is here in Nashville watching me. And there's another spy here too, at Royal Road."

"Don't worry about Fireball."

"What did you do with him?"

I wouldn't tell her I got what I could from him, gave him some false information and he escaped me. I hoped he took the information back to Killer. I was sure he wouldn't reveal what info he gave up to me. He'd get his ass kicked for it.

I focused on something else she said. "Another spy. Who told you that?"

"Killer. You read his texts. You have to read between the lines with him."

I didn't tell her we hadn't recovered them all. "Why would you believe anything he says? I saw that he assured you he'd only be killing the men here. What did you think he'd do with the women and children he found?"

Maren put her hands on her hips. She grimaced. "Honestly, and I am being truthful, I really hadn't thought about it until I got here. I was only following orders. I signed up to prospect." Looking dejected, she wrung her hands. "See, I'm a bit impulsive. Manic, really. But I'm loyal. Frankly, I didn't know what being probate would entail. I didn't know what Killer would demand of me. I thought I was going to be fucking cleaning toilets. And getting hazed. Even doing something illegal but not killing anyone. I had no idea he would send me on a suicide mission. But I know better now. I also know something else, if it doesn't seem like I have you in the palm of my hand, the Gods are likely to kill me off. They have someone here watching me who is likely to take me down. You've got to help me."

"I don't have to do nothing. You think I'm gonna put my whole club in danger for you?"

"Tell them right now then. You said what would happen to me. What the Royal Bastards will do to me. You act like I'm horrible, when this club would do exactly the same to me, the same thing the Gods did to your sister."

After seeing Kingpin kill that nurse, Penelope so easily, without a second thought, I knew the club would have no mercy on a spy even if it was Maren. Prez proved more brutal when it came to his wife and child.

And besides, I'd already planned to use her myself. I knew Killer's plans now. I knew Maren was supposed to call them to our club once I tried to kill her. Therefore, I would make a move when she least expected it. I'd scare her. I'd let her escape with her phone. Let her contact the Gods. But me and my brothers would be ready for them.

Nonetheless with her helping Opry with this damn Halloween carnival, I couldn't do it anytime soon. I'd have to wait until after Halloween. Or fuck, on Halloween. I'd tell my boys to be ready. When the Gods got here, we would kill them instead. I would lure the enemy in just like they wanted, but they all would die.

Maren would be my bait. I'd set my snare, but she couldn't know.

I lifted her chin. My expression tempered. "Maren, you don't know anything about me. I wouldn't do that to you. I wouldn't let my brothers hurt you," I lied. Stepping in close, I seized her in my arms like I had before. "You're not one of them. Not yet. I'll keep your secret for now. But they killed my sister. If I help you, you can help me get my revenge on them."

Her body collapsed against me. "Oh, thank god. I'll help you if you continue to play like we're together."

"It's a deal," I said into her soft hair. I couldn't trust her.

I knew something else after interrogating Fireball. There were enough Asphalt Gods in the area to be here quickly. I just needed Maren to throw them off my scent.

Taking a step back, I studied her face. She'd bought my act. I gave her back her phone.

"Good. If I don't answer Killer every day, he'll send in the Calvary," she said.

"Tell Killer I'm on track to fall in love with you or whatever. But I haven't yet. You plan to break my heart after Halloween night, November first. I'll tell my boys that morning to be ready for them."

"Why wait?"

"I don't want to ruin Prez's party. You're helping with that right?"

Maren nodded.

"Man needs cheering up. We all do. And I'm not gonna let you out of my sight. Whoever this spy is at Royal Road, they're going to think I'm falling in love with you because you're going to spend every night in my bed."

"Don't expect me to fuck you again."

I captured her again. Maren responded best to threats. It made her pussy wet. I'd use it to my advantage. She'd be eating out of my hand come November.

"Oh, you will. You stray from the plan, I'll know. I will kill you if you betray me. And if I ever have to be away from you, even for one second, you should know I have some allies I can trust. I have whores here who will do anything to please me. They'll all have eyes on you now after your stunt this morning, leaving the property. You're not to leave again. You got that?"

"I got it," Maren said, breathlessly, convincingly.

"And don't go thinking I won't be fucking your pussy for real. Because if I'm not fucking you, I'll be fucking one of the whores, and then your spy will know you're not doing your job."

Maren trembled in my arms, and I couldn't wait to have her tonight.

For now, I had to let her go back to Opry and make their Halloween carnival plans. As I sat at the bar, drinking whiskey, I thought of my own plans to have as much fun with her as I could before I betrayed her. And killed her whole club.

Morgan Jane Mitchell

CHAPTER 11

Levi

After weeks in the hospital with Kingpin being back at Royal Road felt better than ever. Especially since Prez was occupied. Knowing he had absolutely no plans and Pagan was still partly acting as Prez with Villain protecting him, I had rare time off.

Also, I had something to look forward to, playing with my new toy, Maren. I threw back a drink with Horror as she distorted her body on the stage, impressing everyone. I watched her with a lot more pride until I remembered she wasn't really mine. Strangely, noticing all the men's eyes on her felt different than before. What if someone else found out she was a spy? She'd be dead meat and there would be fuck all I could do about it.

"That girl there is a vision," Horror said at my side.

His gruff voice made him sound sinister, but he was a softy. Since he'd be gone romancing his new woman, I'd be taking Maren back to his place tonight to keep up our act. And to have my way with her again.

"You're one lucky son of a bitch. Does Chloe know?" He asked, ruining my thoughts.

"Know what?" I didn't want to talk about my estranged wife.

"That you're claiming another woman?"

Hell. That was a problem I hadn't thought about.

"Not any of her business. Or yours."

"Whole club heard Maren told Opry she's yours. Tonya's Chloe's neighbor now. Word is bound to get to her about this. You ready for Chloe to come here showing her ass?"

"Why would she? I've fucked every whore in this joint, and she knows it."

I dared her to, after what she did to me and me still supporting her and her kids.

"But you've not said a woman is yours before besides her. Plus, you're still legally married," Horror kept reminding me.

"You know something I don't, Horror? I know you've been staying over there."

"It's my house. I only put Tonya in it for that purpose. I know Chloe's been saying she's going to do something."

"What?"

"Beats me. I can only assume. Better warn her off it."

Fuck. I'd have to. But I wouldn't think of it tonight.

Horror distracted me, and I about missed Maren's show. When she went to the dressing room, I followed her. I couldn't wait. I spun her around before she could put on her top.

"Levi, what do you want? I'm getting dressed."

"The hell you are, we're pretending you're mine. I'm going to take you right here." I went for my belt.

"The fuck you are, my pussy's too sore from last night."

"Get on your knees," I commanded.

"Right here in the dressing room? Someone could come in on us."

Fuck. That was even hotter. "Good enough for Hallow but not good enough for me."

"You want me to give you a list of men and what I've done with them so you can one up them."

"No, I want to shut you up with my dick, so open wide."

Crossing her arms, Maren huffed.

"You want to look like we're fighting?"

"No," Maren said with a pout that wasn't at all sincere.

I took her by her hair and forced her onto her knees.

She whimpered, loving me dominating her. Staring up at me with a sultry expression, her hands went to release my cock.

She muttered, "I thought we were going to your place to do this."

Her lips landed on my cock. Fuck. Watching her kiss it only made it harder.

"We're going to Horror's place, where I'm staying. Don't worry we have it all to ourselves until Halloween."

"You don't have your own place," she asked between licks.

I fought a moan as she worked her magic. "I did. I lived with Goliath. Now Eve is staying there."

"I don't know why she won't perform on Halloween. She says she's sick. She's been throwing up for a month."

"You think she's pregnant?"

"I don't think she's with anybody. I don't think she's back with Hallow."

"You just wanted to say his name didn't you, remind me I saw him with his dick in your mouth. Get me angry."

Maren's teeth grazed my dick. I stared down at her.

Gazing up at me, she had an evil grin on her face that answered my question. Her head dipped down to my balls.

"That's the only man I've been with here, besides you, and you are so jealous," she teased me.

And she was right.

"Hell yeah, I'm jealous. You haven't had my dick in your mouth, yet. Why don't you quit licking my balls and get to it."

"Your monster of a dick will barely fit in my mouth."

Fondling her face, I ran my thumb over her wet lips. "You do have a tiny mouth."

Maren was tiny, short with all the right curves. She had the body of a gymnast. And her pussy was so tight.

"You've swallowed a sword before, haven't you?"

With a wicked sparkle in her eye, Maren opened wide. Her mouth opened wider than it should, almost looking unnatural but erotic at the same time. Straining her neck, she about swallowed my dick whole. Like a pelican gulping a fish, she took my cock deep into her throat. Squeezed by her esophagus, I instantly came. Maren gulped. I heaved my dick out of her throat as I squirted. Still on her knees, Maren took my softening member and shoved it back in my pants.

"I can't believe you did that. I've never had a woman able to take me down her throat before."

"I've had a lot of practice. With swords and shit, not with monster dicks. But I guess it translates. Can I get dressed now? I need a drink."

I wanted to take her straight to Horror's place but there was nothing there to drink.

"Get dressed. You deserve that strawberry margarita."

Maren pulled on her jeans and t-shirt and hung up her costume. She went to pull off the stick-on rhinestones.

"Leave them on for later."

We went out into the club, to the bar to get her a drink. Louise who usually stripped was pouring shots tonight. The stick thin brunette smiled broadly when she saw me. The whore was one of my favorites, able to take all of me and more. It'd been a while since she warmed my bed, but she was a freak in the sheets. The barstools were full, so I went up to the end of the bar and told her I needed Maren's drink and a double shot of whiskey for me.

"Leviathan, where have you been? I'm off in an hour if you want to catch up." Louise wrapped her long fingers around my wrist, reminding me she liked to use the shackles.

Before I could answer her, Maren stepped in front of me.

"Back off whore. This is my biker."

"This you, Levi?" Louise asked.

Putting my arm around Maren's waist, I tried to introduce them.

Louise stalked off.

Paisley slid down the bar and filled our order. "Look at you two. Quite the couple."

Maren hung on me like she was climbing a tree, selling the lie. I loved it. We took our drinks over to a booth. Maren slid in first and I sat beside her.

"You know they say if a man sits beside you and not in front of you at a table, he doesn't want to look at you," she said.

"Who wouldn't want to look at you? How can I put my arm around you if I sit over there?" I did just that. "Good job at the bar, acting like you're mine. But don't take it so far."

If she acted like that she wouldn't have to worry about another spy. Chloe would be here in no time trying to kill her.

"Why not? You and I are serious, right?" Maren asked, keeping up the con.

"You're a good actress, huh. As good as you are a dancer?" I said, actress because I couldn't say liar or spy.

"Yes, I am."

"I'm not," I said. I wore my emotions on my sleeve. Anger mostly. That's why everyone feared me. One of the many reasons.

Maren put her hand on my upper thigh like she owned me.

"What would you do tonight if I were really yours and we were having a drink?" she asked.

"You don't want to fuck me on the table, do you?"

Maren let her drink fall on the table hard. "How about you go get me another drink?"

I'd not even started on my whiskey. "I'm not leaving you here."

"It'd look ridiculous if I went with you."

"Wait a minute and we'll get up and go to the bar, I see some empty stools now."

"Yeah, whatever Paisley gave me has worn off. I thought that alcohol would help."

"Planning to get drunk?"

"Maybe. I haven't let myself since I've been here."

"Why not?"

"Had to keep alert. Now you've caught me, I can let loose."

I wasn't above getting Maren drunk especially if she was down.

"Here, take my whiskey. I'll go get us a bottle. Don't move a muscle."

I returned with her margarita, a bottle of Dickel and another glass.

Maren finished the whiskey already.

"Let's play a game," I said, pouring two shots.

"A drinking game?"

"Duh," I said, sliding hers over. "I ask you a question, and if I think you're telling the truth, I'll drink. If I think it's a lie, you drink."

"And what about me?"

"Same rules for you."

"But how will we know for sure what's true?"

"We won't"

"You go first," Maren said, holding the shot glass to her lips. Getting her drunk was going to be easier than I thought.

Morgan Jane Mitchell

CHAPTER 12

Levi

"How many dicks have you taken?"

"Like at once?"

"No, not like it once. Like all together in your whole life."

"I don't know. Five."

"That's A lie. Drink."

Maren took the shot. And then she said, "Oh yeah, maybe six or seven. Ten. Shit, I mean, I am twenty-eight years old. It's a pretty conservative amount, right? Don't you think?"

"I'd say. Your turn."

"I really thought these questions were going to have something to do with a certain situation that we shouldn't even speak about in the bar."

"And that's why they're not. No one here can know what we can't say."

"Exactly. If your brothers found out now. What would they do to you?" She poked my shoulder. Maren was already feeling the liquor.

"Pipe down. Let's slow it down, and let's keep it light. It's a night off for me."

"Oh, sorry."

"Next two questions start when the song changes."

"Sounds good," she said.

My arm around her, Maren and I enjoyed the live music. A cover band played newer tunes I didn't recognize. The bar was jammed and as lively as always. We disappeared in the noise and neon lights.

The song changed, and Maren piped up. "I've got my question. How many women have you been with?"

"I have no idea."

"You have to answer it. I did," she whined.

"That is the answer. A truthful one. You need to drink."

Maren took another shot.

"My turn again. Why did you pick a Hallow of all people?"

"I thought we were keeping it light."

"Answer it."

"He was as drunk as Cooter Brown. I needed to do something to let you know that I was... Available."

Without a word, I took the shot.

"Does that mean you believe me?"

"Maybe."

Maren sipped her margarita as we enjoyed the next song. Right on time she said, "Would you want me, like for real if we weren't, you know, pretending?" she whispered the last part.

"I'd fuck you. Yeah."

"I believe that. Does that mean I need a drink?"

"Yes," I said. Poured her another shot.

My turn. "You been with any other man here?"

"No. But I did see Opry's dick. It looked just like him. It was the weirdest thing, almost like it had a little cowboy hat on."

I had a shot up to my lips, but I about spit into it, laughing.

"When?" I asked her, taking the shot. Having seen Opry's skinny dick. I knew she was telling the truth.

"Right before you came back from the hospital, I told him that I was yours so he would stop waving it at me."

"Whose turn is it?" I said, laughing.

"Oh, it's mine," Maren said, slurring her words. "You said you'd never love anybody again. Do you think I could have fooled you? Made you fall in love with me?"

"No."

"Well, that's just rude. I don't believe you. Take a drink."

"But it's the truth."

"I don't think so. I'm fucking gorgeous. If you didn't find me out, you would've fallen for me, hook, line, and sinker. Take the motherfucking drink."

I poured the shot.

Maren held it up in my face. "Those are the rules. I think you're lying. I think I would have changed you."

"I'll never change. Not for anybody. My turn. Has everything you've done all been an act?"

Maren thought for a minute. "No. I couldn't fake those orgasms."

I laughed again and took another drink.

"My turn. My turn," Maren said. "What would you do if you were me? In my situation? Fuck. We're supposed to be keeping it light."

"I'd run away from a man like me. Run really far away. Hell, you should never be in this situation. I plan to keep you for these next two weeks and fuck you. And there's not a damn thing you can do about it. You're lucky that you enjoy it. There's no way in hell you should have ever let yourself get in this situation."

"Well, that was dark. But I agree with that." Maren took a drink.

She was plastered. Having started drinking before her tonight, I'd gotten to that point too but didn't realize it until I turned my head and the room spun.

Maren shouted, "But there will be no fucking tonight. My pussy is sore. You wore it slap out. Your monster dick. And as much as I loved it, I can't take it again."

"You loved it?"

"No."

"I don't believe you. You just said it. You have to take a drink. And don't fake throwing up again."

Maren took the drink. "You knew I was faking?"

"Not at the time. I do now because you're no light weight. And watching you swallow my dick back in that dressing room, I see you're pretty talented."

Maren took another shot.

"I don't think it's your turn," I said, taking the glass from her.

Maren clutched either side of her head. "I think we need to stop drinking. What do you think?"

"Is that a question? Is it your turn?" I said, not knowing what I said.

Maren said, "Yes. You have to answer."

"No, we shouldn't stop drinking."

"I think you're lying. You need to take a shot."

"I can't. Do you wanna get out of here?" I asked her.

"Does this count as a question?"

I had to think about it really hard. I was fucking wasted. All of the alcohol was starting to hit me at once. Enforcer and usually guarding my Prez, I usually didn't let loose and let this happen.

"Yes, it's a question," I decided a whole minute later.

"What was the question again?" Marin laughed, her chortle seeming to go on forever.

And I guffawed at it. And I don't know how long it took for her to answer my question, but she wanted to dance. I followed her onto the dance floor like a lost puppy. We moved in a haze of alcohol induced euphoria.

Eventually we left Royal Road, headed to Horror's house, where I was staying. But on the way there Maren asked me about Kingpin's place. We found ourselves stopped in front of it.

"Why was it so big? Why does one man need to live in such a big building?" Maren asked, full of theatrics as if she was in a Shakespearian play.

We were both still drunk as hell.

"What the hell does he have in that house?" She got in my face, making it seem sinister.

I answered her. "Well. He has a pool. He has a hot tub. He has a bar downstairs. A small one. Upstairs he has his residence and some apartments. A music room, but not like any normal music room. He has a grand piano. And his equipment. And a little recording booth that from my knowledge no one has ever used."

"He has all that in there. And nobody is using it?" she said, like that was the biggest crime.

"We used to have a lot more parties there. It was kind of, you know, a more intimate place for us club members to have fun. That wasn't till his new Ol' Lady. She's a bit jealous. I'm sure he's gonna grow tired of that."

"You know what we should do?" Maren whispered before she almost tripped.

I caught her. "What?"

"We should sneak in there. Tonight. Go skinny dipping."

"No, we are not bringing anything about this to Kingpin's attention right now. If he found out about you, I don't know what I'd do."

"Oh, you're afraid one of your brothers are gonna kill me and you're going to lose this easy pussy?"

Somehow, we made it back to Horror's place. Next thing I knew I was standing in his living room.

"Speaking of easy pussy," I said.

"I told you even if I were okay with you fucking me until Halloween, I am seriously too sore for all that. I thought that alcohol would help, but it doesn't. I need something a lot stronger."

I didn't have anything like that. I stayed away from those sorts of drugs.

"I've got something that might help." I pulled a joint out of my vest and lit it for her.

She took a hit off it. I did too.

"Okay, let's say that I give your pussy a break. Because I'm a good guy," I bargained with her.

"You're a good guy?" Maren asked. "You're a fucking monster. Leviathan. Oh, he's gonna fucking kill you when he finds out about you."

"No, I'm a good guy. I used to be a good guy."

"But you'll never change," Maren mocked me.

It's something that usually wouldn't fly, but I was way too bombed to care. There was only one thing on my mind, the one thing I had been imagining since I saw this woman.

"What are you imagining?" Maren said.

I hadn't realized I was speaking out loud.

"But you are talking out loud," Maren said.

And that was how well-oiled I was.

"There's something you could do for me. You could give me a private show," I said on purpose.

"I think I'm way too shit faced for that."

But I didn't care. Attacking her, but in a good way, a sexual way, I wasn't going to give her a choice. Maren seemed enthralled with my actions, with me. She delighted in me acting like the monster I was. The more I scared her, the thirstier she got.

Somehow, we were both naked. And I couldn't tell you what happened to our clothes. I bent her. She contorted herself backwards, grabbing her ankles. She came up, her head between her thighs. Somehow, I got my dick between her lips. My hand went to her pussy, and I split it open, sticking my thumbs inside as I fucked her mouth. I came down her throat again.

The next morning, I woke up on the floor, naked.

Maren roused. She was bare too.

Holding her head, she complained she needed coffee.

The carpet was wet around us.

"What in the world did we do?" I asked.

Morgan Jane Mitchell

CHAPTER 13

Levi

"I don't remember at all. I was too drunk," Maren whined. "I've done been bit, chewed up and spit out. I'm too old for this. I feel horrible. I don't want a hangover."

I sat up, but my movements were slower than molasses. Like the undead, we got dressed. We eventually went to Royal Road and found some coffee. Taking it outside to the crisp air, we sipped it by the rows of motorcycles parked out front.

"Do you know what I usually do when I'm hungover? Go for a ride."

"About that," Maren started. "When you caught Fireball, what did you do with the motorcycle? Because that was my Harley."

"You're shitting me?"

"No, it's mine, and I would really like to have it back."

I wouldn't tell her he escaped me. "You think I'm gonna give you a motorcycle? A way to leave? When you're a fucking spy for my enemies?"

Maren gave me a mean glare. "I want my hog back."

We were both in a terrible mood.

"I'm going for a ride. You know I can't go riding without you. So. You can ride on the back of mine."

Begrudgingly, she agreed.

The ride in the cool morning air woke us both up more than the coffee had. And actually, the silent ride was even nicer with a woman's embrace at my back. When we stepped back into Royal Road, Pagan called us into Kingpin's office.

"What's going on with you two? What the hell have you done, Levi?"

Holy shit, did he know about us? Did he know I was keeping the fact that Maren was a spy from my brothers all so I could enact my revenge?

Maren looked terrified. I put my arm around her and felt her tremble against me.

My brothers were going to kill her. I truthfully didn't know what I was going to do. Half of me wanted to knock Pagan out, take her and run. Flee on my hog. I didn't want what happened to my sister to ever be done to her.

When I didn't answer him, Pagan turned around. He turned on the television.

Fuck. I'd forgotten all about the cameras around here. Did they pick up our conversations about Maren being a spy? There were also cameras in the basement. Shit. How could I be so stupid?

"We've got night vision. Levi don't be so stupid," Pagan said, like he could read my mind.

"What are you talking about?" I asked, like I truly didn't know, but I was just buying some time. The video started, so I tried to make it out. What was happening on the screen?

Maren kept quiet as a mouse but looked curious as well.

I squeezed her arm to try and reassure her that I had her back.

Pagan said, "I know it's you, too. Someone saw you two running out of there buck-naked last night."

Last night?

I stared at the screen. The black and white and green figures looked like they were flying. It made no damn sense.

"What am I looking at here, Pagan?"

"Let me turn this up," he said.

"Marco," my voice sounded.

"Polo," Maren's voice came next before her long-drawn-out cackle.

The sound of splashing commenced.

Pagan barked, "Seriously sneaking into the Big House to go skinny dipping in the dark. Any other time I would find it fucking hilarious. But we're all walking on eggshells around here, Levi."

131

Thank fuck that was all it was. Relaxing, I stopped gripping Maren's arm.

Pagan wasn't finished chewing me out. "Kingpin's on his last marble. Man's about to go crazy. Therefore, I'm not gonna tell him about this. I'll erase this video. I already had Sweet Tea go in there and mop up the mess you two made, before he saw it. One of you peed right beside the pool."

I didn't tell Pagan I couldn't remember it. But I did ask Maren if she did once we left the office.

"Hell no. I don't remember a fucking thing. But my hair was really damp when we woke up this morning."

That night after Maren's show, we did not drink a drop. We were both too sick. And unfortunately, we were both too queasy for sex.

"Believe it or not, I just want to sleep for a week," I said as Maren crawled into bed with me. I cursed the whiskey. "I'm sure we'll feel better tomorrow night. And you'll take this big monster dick again."

"Did I call it that?"

"Yeah, you did," I said, letting her lay against me.

We fell asleep almost instantly.

The next morning, Maren was up before me, showered and ready for the day. She told me she had to run to town with Opry. I didn't want her to. Especially since I knew the biker showed his dick to her. And he'd asked me about her before. There was always the possibility she could run off, as well.

But when it came down to it, I really had no other option but to agree, or I would be giving us away.

While she was gone, I had nothing better to do. My mind on her, I went to the basement. I found a range of sex toys. Maren complained about my monstrous dick. About being too sore to take me again. But I was bound and determined. I even grabbed a butt plug, the one with the remote. Just thinking about her wearing it onstage and me controlling the vibration hardened me like never before.

For the first time since my sister was murdered, something occupied me except club business and my quest for revenge. Like a horny teen all I could think about was all the ways I could shove my dick in the sexy contortionist, and now shove other things. She was in for a surprise.

After her performance, when we got back to Horror's place, we were both feeling much better, no longer hungover, or sick.

"There's nothing stopping me from fucking you again now."

Maren said, "Well, where do you want to do it? On the couch, in the bed, on the floor, in the bathtub?"

She was mocking me.

"I mean, I'm just here for your pleasure. Right?"

"You bet your sweet ass, you are." I snatched her and carted her to me. "Let's try that little private performance you were doing for me again. I barely remember it. And I plan to put it in my spank bank and use it every time I whack off for the rest of my goddamn life. So, I need to see it again."

The woman responded to my demands.

Maren hadn't changed out of her costume this time. Therefore, I got to watch her strip for me first, taking off everything. This alluring woman seduced a man who already wanted her, making me crave her unbelievably more.

Though, her movements were raunchy and downright pornographic, they were personalized, with my name on them.

"You're stunning," I said. "Beautiful."

Unlike on stage, the woman actually blushed. I scooped her up and stole her to the bedroom. Told her to finish her act on the bed.

"It's a bit spongy. I do need solid ground, so I don't fall."

Resolved to have her in this bed tonight, I said, "Just do your best."

Maren laid back and showed me something new. Taking her feet one by one, she put them clear behind her head. Then she put her arms in front of her legs. In the position, she splayed her sex out, waiting for me.

"You said you wanted a pretzel," she remarked, her voice dripping with lust.

Fuck. I slipped out of my motorcycle vest and tore off my shirt. Undoing my pants, I got completely naked in a flash.

My dick was ready to dive into her exposed hole. Hot damn, I was going to get to fuck Maren like a pretzel.

"You ready for this monster?"

"I'm not sure," she said, chewing her lip. "Just don't ruin my pussy too bad."

"I won't because I intend to fuck it every night."

Until I betrayed her.

"You understand?" I asked her.

Maren didn't utter a syllable. She swallowed hard. The expression on her face said it all. The thought both terrified her and electrified her. Girl couldn't wait.

As I took her hips, she stayed in the pose. I got the head of my dick right in her. Right away, I knew I wouldn't need any lube. Girl gushed for my big dick. Over her, I heaved her body towards mine as I surged forward, spearing her onto my dick. Trying to.

But like before it was taking way too much effort to fill her to the brink. I was going to hurt her badly if I did. Her pussy was merely too tight for the likes of me and my monster. Maren was too tense. Though the sensation was maddening, I pulled out.

"Hold on. Don't move," I said.

I'd prepared for this.

I got to the ground, under the bed where I stashed the dildos. Getting a handful of them, I joined her. On my knees,

I met her eyes. She was interested as I held out the eight-inch purple wand.

"What are you going to do with that?"

"Does it look more your size?" I was sure the woman could get her small hand around it, unlike my cock. "I'm gonna loosen you up. Fuck you with this first so you can take this monster."

Took no time to shove that dildo up her pussy. It slid right in with no problem. I dragged it out slowly and propelled it back in as far as I could go.

Maren's titillating moan drove me wild.

And I continued, watching it slog in and out of her gash, out of her tight sleeve, it coming out all juicy, fuck. I stroked myself. My hand was big enough to get around myself. I had massive hands.

Then I got a better idea. I went around her, hanging my dick and balls over her little mouth. She could pleasure me while I fucked her hole with the dildo.

Maren nibbled my dick as I relaxed her twat, just teasing me. I knew I couldn't widen her pussy in one night, but she came, and I knew from experience that alone would make it easier for me to enter her. I yanked my dick from her wanton kisses.

"Stay like this," I said.

I didn't want her to move out of the tempting position.

I went back around and got on top of her. Her ankles behind her head, I tried again to stuff my dick in her. It was easier this time to ram her. She took me a lot better. But still screamed as her pussy squeezed my dick like a cobra. I yanked out of her again.

"Get up on your knees," I said.

Maren untangled herself and obeyed me.

I got behind her. Shoving her back forward, I pressed her face to the mattress. With her ass in the air, I stabbed that dildo up her cunt again. Really went to town on her with the wand. Before long, she was screaming again. And once she was, I replaced it with my dick, and I went full force.

Maren wailed.

Forcing my dick into her until it was all the way in, I moved with purpose. Grunting, I beat into her very swollen cunt, doggy style. Then I laid back, taking her pelvis with me, so she could ride me like a reverse cowgirl.

As I examined her ass, bouncing up and down on my dick, Maren leaned over and held onto my ankles as she tried to spring on my big shaft. She showed me her little pink star. Oh, mercy. I observed it as she moved. And as soon as she really started doing it, moving effortlessly, I exploded within her.

But I want more. I wanted up her tight little asshole next where it had to be a million times tighter than her tense pussy.

Holding her sides, I said to her back, "Don't go anywhere." Running my thumb down her ass crack, I stuck it in her velvet pit like a pie.

So goddamn tight and warm.

Maren yelped, "Oh, now you're not doing that."

"Stay still." I felt around the bed for the right one.

Finding it, I took the butt plug and replaced my thumb, stuck it up her asshole. Thing was tiny enough. She could take it. Wish I had the remote. I slapped her ass and watched it jiggle.

"Now ride me again."

"Are you fucking serious? How are you still hard? Didn't you just come?"

"I can come again and so can you."

"Your big monster just keeps coming back to life," she muttered.

"Yes, it has a thirst for your pussy. You better slay this monster before it destroys your pussy again."

Maren moved again with intent, rising up my dick. Sliding down it she'd land with a slap. The base of my monster became engulfed in her juices. The sloppy mess we made of my dick added to my arousal. Her pussy worked my pole, but I watched from behind, captivated by her ass gyrating. Every once in a while, I took my thumb and shoved the butt plug a bit farther up her pursed drain. Then as she'd moved, it'd creep back out. I'd thrust it back in, imagining getting her to take my monster in her sweet ass.

Repeat.

Maren came again and rushed off my dick. She dragged the plug out of her ass.

"I can't take anymore," she grumbled, lying down on the bed in exhaustion.

I got on my knees over her beautiful face.

"Open your mouth," I growled.

Taking my dick in my hand, I squeezed it, jerked off over her face until I squirted my spunk all over it.

Maren's lips spread, and she caught all she could, licking her lips like she adored the taste.

I wiped my cum out of her eyes.

"Marvelous. You're fucking amazing."

I was gonna have so much fun with this woman.

Too bad it wouldn't last.

Morgan Jane Mitchell

CHAPTER 14

Levi

I woke up on Halloween before sunup, a woman in my arms. For two glorious weeks, when we weren't fucking all night, Maren was either hanging with me, performing or busy working with Opry on the haunted carnival. I couldn't keep as good of an eye on her as I wanted while those two snuck around to interview the freaks and shit. Hire a firebreather. Shop for supplies. They were looking for one of those metal hamster balls big enough to ride motorcycles in. They always had an excuse to leave the premises. And I couldn't stop it or seem suspicious. Even though I found myself jealous as hell.

It was not like Maren was riding bitch with him, they'd leave in a Suburban so they could pick up helium or haul all they needed back to Royal Road. However, I couldn't help but think Opry had an ulterior motive for spending so much time with her. After all, he'd asked me if he could put the moves on her and showed her his dick. But he didn't know she was a spy. I clearly didn't have anything to worry about. Not like I was thinking of staying with her or anything, anyhow.

Even though it'd been a while since I'd been fucking the same woman every night. It'd been nice, waking up and rolling on top of her to have morning sex. Then we'd have coffee and breakfast and her and Opry would leave. I'd go check in with Kingpin and he'd be much the same, just spending time with his woman, fretting over her and his unborn twins. Maren and Opry would get back. Maren and I'd eat lunch, go home, and have afternoon sex, maybe watch a movie, go for a motorcycle ride, come back, party at the clubhouse, shoot some pool with my brothers. I'd have dinner with Maren, watch her perform, and then go have sex all night.

That'd been my life for a whole two weeks.

It'd been fucking amazing.

I did however offer to take her out at dawn the morning of Halloween to pick up pumpkins for their carnival.

Opry seemed upset not to be joining her.

I'd never seen the woman so excited as we piled as many gourds as we could fit into the pickup truck. While we were at the orchard, Maren insisted we stay for warm apple cider and donuts.

"This what Opry and you have been doing?" Having little dates.

"We grab a bite when we're out, yeah."

"But you come back and eat lunch with me?"

"It's just small things. And a girl has got to eat as much as we're fucking. Besides, I can't survive on that slop at the clubhouse, no offense to Sweet Tea or any of the cooks."

"Opry's putting the moves on you."

"No, he's a complete gentleman."

That was worse. He wanted more from Maren than a quick fuck. I was more than envious.

Though I had my coffee black, and drank it quickly, Maren savored her drink, marveling at the sunrise.

"Just think, tomorrow this will all be over," she said. "If your club defeats mine, you think Kingpin will let me stay?"

"If?"

Having a different plan, I had no answer for her. I'd decided I didn't want Maren to suffer. That I was sure of, but I planned to have the Asphalt Gods come tonight. And as much as I wanted to, I couldn't trust her. I needed her to call in her gang to rescue her from my wrath later, so for now, I intertwined my fingers with hers.

"I hope he does," I said, it would be the truth if what she thought was going to happen was real.

She thought we were waiting for tomorrow. But in actuality, I would break her heart tonight. When she called the Gods to us, they'd believe she was in serious peril. Maren would believe that I was going to kill her. They'd believe it was time even though they planned for tomorrow.

Back at Royal Road I left Maren to the pumpkins. I'd gotten back in time for our special meeting. We let Kingpin know about the Halloween Carnival like it was Christmas morning. All the officers waited for him in the clubhouse to give him the news. Pagan woke him up early. He came into Royal Road in his black silk robe and nothing else, not even shoes.

The Ferris wheel already arrived before he got up, and men were setting it up. Naturally, he erupted into a million questions before Pagan and Opry could explain. The rest of us were merely flies on the wall, especially me.

As I'd predicted, the biker was none too happy about his surprise.

"Does everyone know but me? How could you do this Pagan? Keeping secrets."

"Prez, we couldn't tell you. That's how a surprise works."

"What about the orgy?" Kingpin scrubbed his face because he was half asleep. "We're famous for it."

"Still happening at midnight." Pagan explained the whole plan to Kingpin. "The family friendly part only lasts from two until the sun sets at seven pm. That part is one hundred percent outside around the tent."

"A tent?"

"A big top. It's a haunted carnival."

"No animals," Kingpin said, snappishly.

"We've got some ponies already on the way."

"This place is going to stink to high heavens for months. You boys know, plenty of events I hold are family friendly. Why take Halloween from me? You know how close it is to my dark heart."

"I figured with you having twins soon you'd understand us who want to spend Halloween with our kids,"

Pagan said. "This way we're able to do that and still have our wild party afterwards. We have a Ferris wheel, a funhouse and carnival games with prizes for the youngins and better still, for the teens and Ol' Ladies, Beau Strick is performing."

"My fucking brother?"

"I thought you two buried the hatchet because of Sky and her mom."

Fuming, Kingpin only crossed his arms. Clearly the feud continued. He'd never get over the fact his Country Music star brother used his name and life story to claim his fame.

Pagan ignored this obvious fact. "For the adults we switch over. We'll start the real party at eight like always. Party 'til the sun comes up. It'll be better than ever. We'll get rid of Bubba and get some real musicians on stage. Got Jackie's Heros coming. Maren performs, of course and a whole host of others like her. The freaks show up, too."

"Freaks?" Kingpin was curious.

"Yeah. You're going to love it."

"Bearded lady?" Kingpin guessed.

"No, something better, and just for after hours. All the carnival games switch up. Bobbing for booty with peaches. Titty balloons for darts. Eggplant balloons filled with cream for the ladies. That was Leo's idea. We're having burnout contests."

"What about the masquerade?"

"Just wait. All the strippers are dressing like killer clowns after the kids leave. The bikers are all dressing up too. Inside we'll have our candy buffet as usual with a whore covered in Halloween candy with your sign that says you must use your mouth. Just like before. Fuck, Buzzard even made sure there's drugs in that candy."

Hearing all the craziness we had planned, Kingpin warmed to the idea.

Thinking about how I was going to tell them about the Asphalt Gods MC sniffing around, I could barely pay attention to it all. Forget raining, I was getting ready to take a big dump on their carnival. I kept listening for the right moment to interject until they started talking about Maren.

"Was this her idea?" Prez asked. "Because I'm not sure I trust that girl. Circus folk can't be trusted. Big Top Eddie killed twenty-one men with a single hammer."

Kingpin was on about some serial killer he met in prison.

"Something's off about her," he said. "Could Maren be our spy?"

I froze. I had to force myself to breathe normally. I wouldn't give her up to them. Not now. Not like this.

"No. It's all my idea. She's only helping," Opry said, defending her.

"Leviathan," Kingpin said. He rarely called me Levi. "You've gotten close to Maren. Can we trust her? Is this circus of hers some kind of deception?"

"We can trust her," I lied, although his question rang in my head. I filed it away for later and kept my face as straight as I could.

Kingpin screwed his eyes and cocked his head. Fuck. I knew I shouldn't underestimate him. Anyone who did ended up dead.

"You're spending all your time with her. You're in love with this girl," he proclaimed like he'd figured me out.

"No," I said too hastily.

"Fuck that. I can tell." Prez however studied me.

"Maren's alright," I answered. That was true enough.

"Well, alright." Prez easily took my word.

Opry continued, "It's not just about the families. The ticket sales are through the roof. We'll be able to rebuild and host fights again, sooner than we thought."

In true Kingpin form his mood shifted like the wind. He put his arm around Opry.

"Tell me 'bout them numbers."

Just like that, Kingpin was onboard. Our meeting was ending. After he questioned Maren's intentions, I couldn't tell him about the Gods. I'd actually have to wait until tomorrow when everyone was hungover and useless.

"Bikers have to dress up?" Kingpin went on asking questions.

"Of course, not you," Opry told him.

I didn't plan on it either.

Since Maren would be performing, she planned to dress like she did in the circus but with a Halloween twist. For the first time, I let myself look forward to this haunted carnival. A weight lifted at least for today.

That was until Opry was in front of me asking if we picked up the pumpkins.

"You let her out of your bed long enough?"

"Listen cowboy, Maren's my girl. Don't be buttering her up, like you do."

"You've not really laid claim to her. No property patch, as I see it. You're just playing around as usual. At least she doesn't think it's too serious."

"She say that?"

"No. But I can tell when a girl's open to something better," Opry said, obviously meaning he was better than me.

"You're playing too. You don't quit making eyes at her, I'll make you disappear."

"What you going to do, sink me in the Cumberland River like the last man you killed for Kingpin?"

"Yeah, but Kingpin will never know."

I left the meeting to go find Maren and help her unload the pumpkins. I discovered her talking to someone.

Shit.

"What the hell are you doing here, Chloe?"

CHAPTER 15

Levi

"Chloe?" Maren asked. She hadn't even realized she was talking to my wife.

"Hi, dad." My daughter, Haven poked her head around a heap of pumpkins and waved.

Her hair matched the pumpkins. She looked just like her mom, freckles and all. But like an ordinary teen in ordinary clothes, shorts too short and an oversized sweatshirt. She held up a bag explaining to Maren she'd be in costume later.

"Oh, what as?" Maren asked her.

"A dark fairy," Haven answered, hauling out the black fabric to show her.

Chloe dressed like the biker bitch she'd always been with too tight denim, black boots, and fake titties you could sit your beer on. They practically popped out of a low-cut Guns and Roses t-shirt. Her ginger hair was pulled back in a tight French braid, and she had on every ring she owned. A Marlboro Light hung from her lips. I couldn't tell if she was already in costume or not. Most of the bikers would end up coming as bikers after all.

Chloe barked at me, "I'm dropping off Haven early to set up the carnival. She drove me here. You need to take her driving before she leaves. If you're going to stick around for any time, this time."

"No one told me," I complained, focusing on one of her grievances at a time.

"All the kids her age are helping." Chloe sucked on her cigarette like a joint.

"I messaged you, dad," Haven butted in.

"You said you were coming but not early," I challenged.

"No. I told you I wanted to come early because I'm leaving soon," Haven argued with me.

I scrolled my phone. "You did not."

"On Insta."

Fuck. I was only on Instagram to spy on her. I didn't check my messages.

"It's okay, honey. Your dad ain't been around enough to know it's that time. Haven's off to that prep school come January," her mom said, putting me down as usual. "She's going to stay with my mom first. Don't you remember? She's leaving next month."

Maren continued unloading pumpkins into the wheelbarrow as our family drama played out.

Chloe went on, "I hope you got my text, Levi. You've got the girls this afternoon. I'll be back to drop them off. I have my own plans tonight."

"You won't be at the carnival with them?" Ivy and Angel weren't mine, but at six and eight they didn't know any better. "You'll be back before eight? Can't Haven watch them?"

"You got plans? Well, I do too. It's high time you watch the kids one evening."

"You know I can't do that while I'm working."

"Haven wants to enjoy the part of this party that she can, while she can. She'll watch the girls afterwards. Don't worry, you won't miss a thing. Just drive them home, will ya?"

I scrolled through my phone while she talked. "You didn't let me know."

Chloe kicked the ground. "You didn't let me know you've been shacked up with some other woman. We've not seen you in weeks."

Not wanting to hear this, Haven stomped off.

Automatically, I looked to Maren to gauge her reaction.

Chloe caught on. "This her? You her?" Chloe's voice came in short bursts. She cracked her knuckles.

"Hi, I'm Maren," she tried, offering her hand.

Chloe stared at her hand in disgust before knocking her lights out.

Fucking hell. I should've known with her hair back and rings, she was fixing to fight.

Maren bounced back, fought back and the dust rose around them. It was a real slugfest. Maren kneed Chloe's crotch, turned her and had her in a stranglehold. Chloe elbowed Maren to escape and grabbed her by the hair, trying to sling her to the ground.

I stepped into the middle of their brawl to break them apart and got scratched up. Holding them apart didn't stop them. They both hit me, trying to get to the other. Chloe landed another punch in Maren's face. Maren grabbed her braid. Neither one of them would give up. Bending down, I snatched Maren by her jeans and flipped her over my shoulder and backed away from Chloe.

Holding out my hand, I threatened my wife, "Come over here, and I'll drop kick you."

"I can fight my own battles," Maren hollered while she beat on my back.

Chloe wiped her bloody nose. "You afraid I'll hurt your new whore?"

"Maren's not a whore," I said.

"Well, that's just peachy. Don't you know he's already got an Ol' Lady, bitch."

"Chloe, I don't love you anymore. You know that."

"Forget watching the girls. They're not coming. Keep your whore. You won't see the girls ever again."

"Don't punish the girls over this."

Chloe flipped me off as she walked away.

I sat Maren down on the tailgate of the truck and tried to look at her swollen eye.

"Don't," she said, her voice hoarse.

Easing up my touch, I tried to be gentler as I examined it. "I think you need some ice." She had a black eye, alright.

"Don't," she went on, pushing my hand away from her face entirely. "I don't need you to protect me. I can take care of myself."

"It was a useless battle. I don't want Chloe. There's no need to fight that bitch."

"I've been fighting my whole life and don't need a man to protect me."

"That's what you're mad about? With everything going on, you choose that."

"You wouldn't understand."

I caressed her face even though she didn't want me to. "Make me understand."

Maren shoved me off, hopped down and walked off. The look on her face, she might as well have flipped me off too.

To hell with this, I stomped off too, back to the house for a fucking nap.

Halloween was proving to be a bitch. It only got worse when the family friendly part of the carnival began. I'd just woken from a nap and the fair seemed to have sprung up around me like magic. There was an orange and black striped big top right in the middle of the clearing. It was flanked by a Ferris Wheel and a haunted funhouse that sat way farther away on purpose, a straw bale labyrinth in front of it. Games dotted the perimeter. I smelled a petting zoo before a screech from the sound system about knocked me over. They were setting up for Beau Strick to sing in the tent. I recognized the voice of Dimple, our Elvis impersonator biker doing a mic check.

"Ah, one. Ah, two…"

The grounds were packed with members and their Ol' Ladies and kids, but also strangers who came for the festivities. Not just our normal clientele either. They'd brought their families. We were all to be on our best behavior for this shit. None of the adults were in costume yet. Only the kids.

Finally finding Maren working a face painting booth, I tried to talk to her.

"How you holding up?"

"I'm right as rain," she said, but instantly added, "It'd be nice if you had volunteered to do something." She painted a crude unicorn on a tiny girl's cheek. I noticed she'd covered up her black eye with makeup, but you could still see it. "We needed help setting up."

"You never asked me to. You ran off."

"If you want to help, meet me in fifteen minutes. I'm just filling in for Paisley who's late. She's the face painter this afternoon and our palm reader later. I really hope she doesn't flake out. I'll find something for you to do."

Maren shooed me away. I walked off aimlessly looking for a brother or two, but everyone seemed to be working.

Then of all people, fucking Fireball walked right on by me. Shit. The Asphalt God who got away from me. I couldn't have been the only one to see him. His face tattoo was a dead giveaway.

Morgan Jane Mitchell

CHAPTER 16

Levi

I followed the rival club member and lost him in the tent. Stepping outside to see if he passed through, I spotted my daughter, Haven getting on the Ferris Wheel with one of Buzzard's grandkids, Adan.

Buzzard was one of our oldest members. Used to be an officer until he was too old to ride much. A high school dropout, Adan was nineteen. What was worse, kid had been begging to prospect. He wanted to become a Royal Bastard. He even wore what looked like his granddad's motorcycle gear as a costume. Haven as always was a beauty even as an evil fairy, but looked too grown up, having on dark makeup and red lips.

Jogging over, I couldn't catch her before she went up and away with the boy. The adult man. The nineteen-year-old. Fuck. Smiling, Haven waved at me from the car. I gave her a knowing look. Adan dunked down to try to hide from me. That little motherfucker knew I didn't want him anywhere near my daughter. I'd threatened him once. I was going to rip his balls off this time.

"How long is this ride?" I asked the operator.

"Twelve minutes."

"I'm getting on this next one," I told him in a voice that dared him to protest.

But the next one was already full.

"Get me on this ride."

"Hold on," he said. "There's one more."

I had to wait for the wheel to make a slow rotation.

"You're cutting line," a girl behind me grumbled.

Turning around, I saw five little girls in regular clothes, not costumes. They couldn't be older than my daughter Angel who was eight. Hell, my girls were missing Halloween all because of Chloe's fit. I had half a mind to leave and go get them.

"What makes you think you can skip in front of us, Boomer?"

"Well, you're supposed to dress up." Having three daughters, I knew how to deal with smart-mouthed little girls. "You lose your spot for that."

"We are dressed up. It's a group costume. What are you?"

"I'm a biker." I tugged on my cut.

"Looks fake," one of them said. "Biker, my ass."

The others laughed. Little girls could be vicious.

Turning my head, I saw their moms off to the side shooting the shit while they waited. Some of these were

Horror's woman, Tonya's kids. That explained the mouth on them.

"What are y'all supposed to be?"

"Think oldies." They gave me a clue.

"An athlete? A singer? A witch? Union Jack t-shirt? What are you, the Village People?" I clapped back.

"We're the Spice Girls," they all said in unison.

Oh, an oldie from the nineties, boomer indeed.

They all made a face, spun their eyes, and continued to eat their orange and black cotton candy.

Someone poked my shoulder, and I turned to see Maren. Thank God.

"Want to go for a ride?" I asked her. The next empty car had finally arrived.

"Sure," she said, like she wasn't too sure. Staring up at the ride, she shook her head. "Actually, I don't have time."

My hands landed on her shoulders, and I rubbed. "You're stressed. You need to unwind. It's only about ten minutes."

She breathed in deep. "Okay, I need a break."

In the next second, we sat in the cart, my arm naturally going around her tiny body. The man closed the gate. We made it halfway around before I could spy on Haven.

"Isn't that your daughter?" Maren pointed in front of us.

Haven was a couple cars ahead and couldn't hear us because Bubba had started singing. Her head was in the crook of that boy's neck.

"Where?" I looked over the side and the whole cart rocked.

"Fucking hell," Maren shouted. "Don't do that. Are you too big to be on this ride?"

Woman panicked.

"You're scared of heights?"

"Not exactly. I took a bad fall on the trapeze. I'm scared of falling to my death. Why are you stalking your daughter?"

"I don't want her to end up like her mom. Pregnant before she's ready."

"I hear you," Maren said like she understood.

"You said you have a kid." It was a question.

"I did?"

"You don't think I remember?"

"You didn't ask anything further."

She was right. I hadn't asked about it at the time. We were in a much different place. I'd just found out she was a spy. I wanted to fuck her but not get all the details.

"Yeah, I did have a kid."

"So?" I expected her to go on.

Maren fiddled with the mood ring on her right hand. "So, I had a kid. I was seventeen. It was the reason I couldn't compete in the Olympics that year. Found out I was pregnant. My career ended then."

"I thought you said you were twenty-one when you stopped?"

"I lied," she said.

Lied? Another lie. But this one felt like a slap in the face for some reason. Maybe because I knew her better now.

"I told the circus company that too. The truth is my mom made me put the baby up for adoption, and I spent three years in a mental institution afterwards. Not sure if they're still called that, but you know what I mean. I was hospitalized for being. Unstable."

"What?" I didn't mean for it to come out like it did, as an exclamation, but it couldn't be helped. With all the talk from Kingpin about carnies being crazy and all.

"That was seven years ago," Maren tried to brush it off.

I tried not to focus on it. But I had to ask, "How were you unstable?"

"I tried to kidnap my daughter from her adoptive parents. Instead of jail, I was hospitalized. It was a dark time for me."

"Where's your daughter now?"

Maren took a minute to answer. "Last time I saw her, Galveston, Texas. But I didn't try to take her again. I'm not crazy. But I was curious. I followed her mom, and she served me a strawberry margarita. My mom made me have her then give up my baby to be raised by a couple who got divorced three months later. She was being raised by a single mom who ended up waiting tables. No offense to her, but how was that any better than me?" Maren stopped abruptly. "I'm sorry. Your daughter seems sweet."

"She is. A little too sweet. She's sweet on that troublemaker there." I pointed at them.

"How about you? Other than the dead sister, tell me how you're screwed up, so I don't feel too mortified right now."

"You shouldn't feel mortified. The things I've done to you, you think you should feel embarrassed? I know the ends and outs of your body. I've been inside you every night for two straight weeks."

"You don't have to tell me."

"What's to tell? My life story? My dad was an alcoholic, and my mother a whore. They split and split me between them, so I focused on swimming. I was fucking good at something, but I knocked up my girl. She's a bitch, you met her."

"Yeah, what a bitch." Maren touched her sore eye, agreeing with me.

"We had a kid too young. I was always on the road and Haven barely had a dad for the first part of her life. Chloe hated me for it. My folks got back together and became Born-again Christians. They disowned me after I was banned from competing and became a biker. Even after I finally married Chloe like they always said I should. Jesus forgave them, but they had no forgiveness for me. You don't want to know what they thought after my sister died how she did. They suspected me. Not that it was my fault, because by all accounts it was, but that I had somehow done it myself. They live right here in Nashville and have never met some of their grandkids."

"That's awful. My dad was an alcoholic too. He used to beat my mom. Mom pretended it didn't happen and lived through my gymnastics. He would beat me too. And I had to fight him."

"That's why you didn't want me to stop Chloe from beating your ass?"

"Your wife? She wouldn't have. And yes, partly."

"You bothered that I'm married?"

"Why would I be? This arrangement. It's not real."

I took her hand. "Things are only as real as we make them," I said, surprising the fuck out of myself.

Maren said nothing.

I changed the subject. "So, who was the dad?"

Maren didn't answer.

"Some young bad boy like that kid riding with my daughter?" I tried again to ask about the father of her baby.

"No."

"Come on. I won't get jealous," I said, playfully kissing her hair. I ran my hand up her shirt.

She knocked it away. "Just drop it."

"Are you okay today?"

"No. I thought I would be. I was really excited about this carnival, but it's just a fantasy." Maren teared up. She wiped her eyes with her long sleeve. "Tomorrow, I don't know what's going to happen or if I'll ever see you again or if I'll even be living."

Her words touched me. Broke my heart. I'd planned to betray her but just so I wouldn't get played. Now, there was no need. I'd stay on alert, and we'd take care of the Asphalt Gods tomorrow like I told her to tell them. I had to trust her because I wouldn't give her over to my club.

Taking her face in my hands, I made her look at me. "I'm not going to let anything happen to you," I said.

I felt the sentiment rumble deep within me. My lips fell to hers, and we kissed for the first time. I'd not even realized until that very moment I hadn't kissed her once on her lips. Maren responded, her kiss so soft and sweet, but not like I thought she would. While I felt fireworks, she was timid.

She pulled away, apologizing.

"No, I'm sorry. You're crying. I shouldn't have," I said.

It was the wrong time.

Maren only cried harder, but she quickly settled. "I'm alright."

I tried to make light of it, to make her smile. "Is this about your baby daddy?" I joked.

"No. You want to know who the father was? My dad."

Bile rose in my throat. Not only did that break my heart. It broke my soul.

"I'm so sorry," I tried, but it would never be enough. I hoped the fucker was dead. If not, he'd be at the top of my list.

"It's okay. It took a long time to get over. It took me a long time to realize I enjoy sex and kinks because I'm an adult with natural needs. It has nothing to do with him or anything else. I don't want to think of it ever again in my life. That's why I don't tell anyone about it. I don't want to have lived it. I didn't want to have his baby of course, but my mother made me lie about the father and have it."

"He live here in Nashville?" I asked, honestly thinking of ending an old man's life. When she didn't answer, I repeated myself, "I'm sorry."

"Just don't say anything, okay. I'm done talking." Maren laid her head on my chest. We finished the ride in silence.

When the ride stopped and we got off, I saw Haven walk off hand and hand with that boy. But I couldn't leave Maren. There were plenty of my brothers who would have an eye out for my daughter.

"Now, what can I help with?" I focused on Maren.

Her mood had improved drastically. "I've got something special for you. Something you'll be perfect for. Just please be a good sport. Remember, it's for the kids."

Maren led me to a large tank of water. "A dunk tank? You expect me to sit in this damn thing?"

"Come on. You'll look great doing it. You've got this sea creature all over you. When a kid dunks you stay under as long as you can then pop up and scare the shit out of them. Okay?"

"You've thought this through? Planned it?"

"The whole time. Please," she begged.

"What will you do for me later?" I said my voice pure sex.

"Anything," she said, like she meant it.

"Anything?"

"Anything, but no butt stuff."

"Okay, but I'll think of what later."

Maren turned to leave.

"Wait. Where are you going? Are you just trying to get away from me?" To betray me, I wanted to ask, but that didn't feel right anymore.

"As much as I would love to stay and witness this, I've got to go check on everyone else. Opry's not doing a damned thing. He's not even speaking to me for some reason. Then I have to get dressed, do my hair and makeup. I go on at eight. I'm the opener for this evening's festivities."

"You'll be free after that?"

"Yes. After that I'm done. I couldn't care less after dark. I'm going to hand over the baton to Memphis. She can run the rest. She wants to, she said."

Nice that Memphis was coming around.

"You can come help me undress."

"I guess I'll catch you at your show then."

Maren turned again, but I caught her.

"What?" She grumbled.

Holding her to me, I brushed back her hair.

She looked at me puzzled.

Maren was so beautiful, inside and out. I'd been all over her, inside her. She had me wrapped around her finger. And she had a hold of my dead heart.

"What else could you possibly want," she droned.

I wanted her. All of her. I wanted her to stay with me, not at the dunk tank, but here at Royal Road. But I had no time to tell her. It was her time to shine. She'd worked so hard planning this party. I'd confess my feelings later.

"You can't leave until you've kissed me."

We kissed, but her smile ruined it and made it perfect at the same damn time.

"You know what's sexier than helping a woman undress? You can come help me dress," she said.

"Like lace up your corset kind of shit?"

"Yeah, that kind of shit," Maren said as she bounced away.

CHAPTER 17

Levi

Kids, my ass.

I was soak and wet from being dunked by everyone in the goddamn club.

Even Prez got in on the action. Since he never dresses up, they gave him a top hat and his whip. After all, he was the ringleader of this circus. His Ol' Lady, pregnant with his twins, was showing and had her belly exposed and painted like a Jack-o-lantern. They were the only bikers already in costume if you didn't count Dimple who always dressed as Elvis. I heard him say, he'd be switching it up for the real party and doing an undead Elvis tonight.

Damn, Kingpin had an arm, and they didn't charge him, so I went under ten times until he got bored with it. Then the man started a bet on how long I could hold my breath. Fuck, he could bet on anything. I entertained him once and won him a pile of cash. But soon, I felt like one of the freaks. I'd had enough. I told Prez I was done. At least the biker respected that.

Memphis joined me beside the tank as I tried to dry off.

"That was Junebug's thing, the Jack-o-lanterns." She spoke of Prez's woman as always.

I nodded. "Yeah, she liked to paint her titties like it every Halloween."

"How could he forget it? Kingpin replaced us with a younger model. Knew it'd happen. Men are all the same. Anyway, where's that Maren of yours?"

Of mine. It did sound nice. Maybe she would be mine if everything went well tomorrow.

"You've not seen her?"

"No, but I said I'd take over so she can do her act."

I had wondered if the head of our whores was being genuine or not.

"You're stepping up again?" I asked her only to get more information.

"Someone's got to. Besides, Opry's not worth shit without me. Royal Road's going downhill. We're having a goddamn kiddie fair for Christ's sake. But tonight, we'll be back to our old evil self. We're doing biker rides, too, my idea."

"What's that?"

"Saddling up some of the prospects to replace the circle of ponies."

"But they'll be in the shit."

"That's the point. You fuckers have gone too soft on them." Memphis laughed.

Memphis reminded me of Maren complaining that we didn't patch women. If anyone deserved a patch in all these years, it was Memphis. She always ran this show.

"The ladies are going to love it. Five bucks a ride's not too much, right? We're making money hand over fist with your girl's idea."

"Maren's idea?"

"This Haunted Carnival. She talked Opry into doing all this cause he's sweet on her."

I was speechless. The carnival was Maren's idea? Kingpin's question from earlier rang through my head. Did Maren plan this for a nefarious reason? All this time, I thought Halloween night would be the perfect time to get the Gods here. Catch them unaware and defeat them but maybe that had been Maren and Killer's plan all along.

"Oh, I almost forgot, I've seen Fireball too," Memphis announced, adding to my worry. "But I'm not too worried about him. Also, thought you should know, Kingpin's allowed another Asphalt God on the premises. Eve's brother, Hob. He's been staying over the clubhouse for weeks now."

What the hell? "I haven't seen him. No one has said."

"No. They don't want to tell you and get him killed. And you've been too busy playing house while Prez doesn't need you. He's keeping a secret for that girl, Eve for some damn reason. Aren't you wary? He gave her your house. She's not even an officer."

"Kingpin?" I didn't want to tell Memphis I suspected our Prez had feelings for that girl even if I hadn't seen any evidence that he'd been fucking her. Perhaps she blackmailed him. None of it made a lick of sense.

"Eve's brother is keeping to himself until Kingpin decides what to do with him, I've heard."

"Could he be our spy?" I tried to throw the scent off Maren but was also curious.

"Doesn't match up with timing, but I don't trust him as far as I can throw him," Memphis said.

With all of that, I had to warn her. I thought of a way to tell her without telling her. "I've got some intel of my own. I ran into Fireball a couple of weeks ago. From what he said, I got a feeling they're about to make a move. The Asphalt Gods MC. All of them. An ambush. If he's here, perhaps it's tonight."

"You didn't report it?" Memphis was instantly apprehensive.

"I tried to tell Prez, but he's been fawning over that wife of his," I lied. "So, I need you to go tell all the men to be on high alert tonight. Have their weapons ready. Tell them to be careful not to get too drunk or high. Be ready for a fight to the death. I hadn't thought of it until now, but this Halloween party would be a perfect time for them to surprise us."

"Agreed. Shit's dangerous. Should I tell Prez?" She thought enough to ask.

I made an executive decision. He'd shut this show down, and we wouldn't be able to wipe the Gods out like I longed to. "No. I already tried. We'll have to keep this secret to protect him. Tell Pagan though and tell him that Kingpin doesn't believe it."

I knew that even with everything that had happened between them, Memphis loved Kingpin. She'd want to keep him safe. She'd spread the word. Gossip was her specialty.

It was nearly seven, therefore I went to find my daughter. I'd have to drive her home. At least with the youngins home, I could take her on the back of my Harley. I could clear my head on the way back. I couldn't quit thinking that possibly Maren was up to something. I couldn't figure out if I believed she was truthful. On the way to search inside the tent, I ran into Thorn.

He flirted with a little person, a gang of them.

Big, black, and wearing a cowboy hat like Opry did, Thorn was our badass Cleaner. He had nary a tattoo on him, except for his backpack, the Royal Bastards logo. But he did have a couple of piercings, some diamond bling in his ears and a bar in his eyebrow. A stone-cold set of eyes adorned his smooth face. The things he'd seen would torture most men. Not just what he'd seen in this club, he was ex-military with stories that even sickened me, the supposed monster.

I greeted him and the little ladies marched off.

"What's with them?"

"The little strippers, your girl hired them for tonight. Ain't that wild?"

"No, I mean, they left awful quick."

"At the sight of you, yeah. You look mean, man. Plus, you've got a reputation around Nashville, you know. No mercy shit."

"I'm merciless."

"Yeah, brother. But you're supposed to be. You're our Enforcer. Not a lowly Cleaner like me. The ladies aren't scared of me because they don't understand what a Cleaner does. They think I'm mopping floors or something. Like I'm the janitor. It's fucking embarrassing sometimes."

Being the Cleaner not only meant he was in charge of the crew cleaning up a crime scene. It meant he hunted down the enemies we missed and killed them indiscriminately.

"Where are you off to?" he asked.

"I'm taking Haven home before the wild party starts."

"Wild is right. They couldn't get a bearded lady, but they did one better. Opry hired a girl who has two vaginas. Can you believe that shit? Two pussies. She's setting up in the basement. It's a look but no touch situation, but I'm going to try and hit that afterwards." Thorn chugged an IPA. "Want to help? There are three holes."

"You and every biker here, I'm sure. But no, brother I don't want to rub dicks with you. Hey, has Memphis talked to you yet?"

"What have you heard? We aren't doing anything but fucking."

"No. I'm not talking about that." I took the time to tell him about Fireball snooping around and my suspicions.

"Fuck, man. I intended to get plastered. Shit faced wasn't the word. Can't now. I see one of them Gods, I'll kill them for fucking with our Halloween."

"That's the spirit," I said as I left to search for Haven.

Searching everywhere, I couldn't find my daughter. I asked Opry, Cricket and Gunn who worked the front gate if they'd seen her leave with anyone.

Opry said, "No. But I did see her with Buzzard's shit of a grandson earlier. They were in the back of one of the cars out front, making out. But I opened the door, told them to get lost."

"Why didn't you bring him to me?"

"Girl's sixteen, almost seventeen, ain't she? It's a party. They weren't fucking. Relax."

I took him by his western style shirt. "Fuck you, Opry. You don't have kids. She's almost seventeen. 'Bout the age you like them. Get your eyes off her, you pervert."

I was fixing to fight him.

"Hold your horses, Levi. We'll find her. There's an hour yet until the youngins need to clear out. She's probably trying to get an autograph before Bubba leaves like the rest of the teens."

Gunn spoke up. "Adan's old enough to stay for the real party, maybe your girl's hiding out, trying to stay too."

That was a real possibility. Sounded like something she'd do. I let go of Opry.

"The hell she will," I proclaimed. "Should've made the age limit twenty-one and over, Opry, but then your girlfriend couldn't come."

"Half the strippers are between eighteen and twenty-one, Levi. You've never complained before. Guess since Maren chose you, you think you're better than us, but she's trash too."

"What did you say about her?"

"She's trash. A fire spinner we hired knows of her. Told me she was a pregnant teen. A real nutcase. Thinks she sees ghosts and shit. Therefore, you don't need to be harping on me liking them young. At least they're not crazy."

"Keep my woman's name out of your fucking trap," I advised him.

Opry stepped up to me, his hands on his hips like he was in a gun fight in the old west. "Make me," he dared me, his hand hovering over his gun.

Clobbering him, I knocked the cowboy hat off his head. Took his gun like it was candy from a baby. It was all too easy to overtake the twig of a biker. But I wasn't planning on hurting him. I needed all the brothers I could get tonight. A little shit talk was nothing, wouldn't distract me from my heap of problems.

Leaving him on the ground, I said, "That was stupid, fucker. Need to warn you boys."

I told them to be on the lookout for the Asphalt Gods MC. They were as disheartened to be on guard as Thorn had been and have to miss some of the fun. But it had to be done.

Opry got up and dusted himself off. "We'll keep an eye out for Haven too. I'll spread the word about both things. She'll show up, brother."

I searched for Haven for the next thirty minutes with no luck. Everyone saw her with that boy, Adan. Finally, I went to find Maren in the dressing room before she missed me.

Haven sat with her.

"What the fuck are you doing here?" I asked her.

Morgan Jane Mitchell

CHAPTER 18

Levi

"Don't talk to your daughter like that?" Maren said, her face made up like a sad mime.

"This isn't any of your business." I spoke to her, gruffly then focused on my kid. "I've been looking for you all over."

Full of attitude, Haven leapt from her seat and said, "I've been looking for you too. Someone told me to ask Maren. So, here I am."

"I told her to wait here," Maren explained, since I knew you'd be coming this way.

"Don't you check your texts, dad?" Haven went on.

"He doesn't," Maren said, agreeing with her.

I glared at her, taking my daughter's side.

"What? I tried to text you too."

I searched for my phone. "Fuck, I left it at the dunk tank," I said, realizing.

Memphis had distracted me so much that I'd not even thought of checking it.

"Anyway, dad. I tried to meet up with you at seven to see if I could go wait in line for an autograph."

"I don't think so."

"My friends are already in line, see," she whined and tried to show me her phone. "They're saving me a spot. It's not eight yet."

"Opry said he found you in a car making out with Adan," I blurted out, accusing her. "You're not to be messing with that boy."

"Dad," she complained. Gesturing to Maren, she made it clear I embarrassed her. "No cap, nothing happened," she added like I knew what that meant.

I made a face that showed my confusion.

"I swear nothing happened," she explained in a way I understood. "And Winnie offered to drive me home."

"I'm taking you home." I wanted to make sure she got there.

"No offense, but since mom didn't go out, I have another Halloween party to be at later. I don't want helmet hair."

"We can take a car." I was nothing but a problem solver.

"Mom already agreed to let Winnie take me, so I'm just doing you a courtesy by even letting you know," Haven came back.

"She did?"

"Yeah, you want to call and check?" she asked, trying to hand me her phone.

"No," I said. "I believe you," I lied. "I'll call your mom from my own phone and make sure you got home safe." I smiled. "If you're not home by nine, I guess I'll be searching for Winnie. Who's she?"

"Only my best friend since forever."

"Oh, yeah. Short green hair?"

"That's her." Haven hugged me. "See ya, dad. Nice meeting you, Maren," she said as she left.

"She's a handful," I said to Maren who looked overwhelmed.

"I've been waiting for her to leave."

"She's not all bad," I started.

"No, Haven is a dear, really. I just need to get changed. I'm running behind." Maren pulled off her shirt.

With her only in a bra, I stopped her. "Is there something you're not telling me?"

All I could think of was how she might betray me, like I had planned to deceive her.

"You can tell, huh? I saw Fireball. I spoke to him. I think he's casing the joint getting ready for tomorrow. He asked if I'd revealed myself to you yet."

"What did you tell him?"

181

"Of course, what you told me to. That I would bait you into trying to kill me tomorrow once I woke up from this wild night we're about to have. He seemed satisfied. He believed me."

"Is that all? Anyone see you talking to him?"

"Hope not. He was careful. He got the better of me, stepped into the porta john right after I did before I could lock the damn door."

"Anything else?"

"In general, or what do you mean?"

I was still wary that she might be betraying me. She might have planned this whole night to take us down. But I couldn't be sure.

"You could tell me about that road name."

Maren sneered and smiled sideways. "Do I have to? Road names are always a bit shit. Nothing but making fun of me."

Reaching behind her, she undid her bra and let it fall away.

I wouldn't get distracted. "Why are you Spooky?"

"It's a long story."

I held Maren's corset in my hands. I held it hostage. I needed to know if she'd tell me the truth.

"You don't have much time until you go on," I reminded her.

Maren blew out, making her lips sound like a balloon deflating. "If you must know, I saw a ghost." She held up her hands. "And before you even think it, this is completely unrelated to the mental ward. It started afterwards the night I fell."

At least she told me the truth although I didn't know how I felt about it.

"You mean, your club is making fun of you because you thought you saw a ghost."

"No. I see them. I talk to them. Not all the time but when they want to."

"Well, that is spooky."

"It's not something you can live down either once someone hears about it. People think I'm crazy. I don't want to talk about it."

With that, I helped Maren with her corset, tightening it as far as it could go. And she was right, it was intoxicating, dressing her. I forgot all about the ghosts and settled on the fact, she'd come clean. Maybe I could trust her. Maybe all the feelings I had for her were real and not for nothing.

Her tits spilled out of the contraption completely. I ran my thumbs over her nipples, feeling them harden instantly.

"You're not wearing a top at all." She usually removed her bra during the show.

"Only these silver pasties." She placed them.

My eyes didn't leave her hands. Maren was doing a disappearing act, stripping in reverse. And I was hooked.

"I'm doing the whole show with them. It's the best of both worlds," she explained.

Somehow, watching her casually dressing was better than a rehearsed show. Intimate. More erotic, but since she was already in sexy clown makeup, curiously hot.

"Not getting naked for everyone?" I asked her.

"No, only for you, later."

I took her hands, held both of them. "Don't take this off first. Let me. Or your makeup. I want to." I wanted her to come to me like this. I'd cum on her face and smear this face paint.

She went on clarifying about the pasties, "My show's more than that tonight. Not just about sex."

Maren stood in just the black waist corset and a thong, and all I could think about was sex with her.

My hands ran over her plump ass and squeezed. "What about the bottom half of you?"

"I have that tutu," she said, pointing to it. Black as well, it had sparkles that matched her silver lined makeup and jewelry.

Taking it, I held it so she could shimmy into it. Running it up her legs, I could barely stand. My dick was rock hard by the time I faced her. I spun her.

"It barely covers your ass," I said, noticing. She usually had on a bigger panty that showed only a little ass cheek, not a tiny thong that left her so exposed.

"Like I said, it's the best of both worlds. No nipples but more to see under the tutu."

"Under it. There's no under it," I objected, running my hands over her thong.

I nibbled her ear.

She protested, "Stop, you're going to get my pussy all wet and that won't be good at all. This thong will slip, and I'll flash everyone."

My hands froze. I stopped teasing her. "I don't want anyone to see my pussy," I breathed in her ear.

"Stop with the dirty talk, too," she begged, biting her lovely black painted lip.

"If it's such a problem, let's take them off."

"There's no time," she grumbled.

There was, for what I planned to do. Reaching under her tutu, I slipped off her thong and picked her up.

"What the hell are you doing?"

"You can't go on stage so horny. You'll have all the men after you. Get on my shoulders. Grab that beam way up there over us, if you can."

I helped her up to the ceiling. Her legs went over my shoulders where she was facing me, her pussy in my view. I breathed her in. She smelled of sweet and spicy sex. In nothing but the corset, she hung from the rafters like she was performing. I stuck my tongue between her wet folds.

Aroused for me, Maren tasted luscious. Grasping her ass, I licked her gooey pussy like I was eating an ice cream cone they were selling just outside. She tasted of salty, warm, raw desire all for my monster sized dick. Cooing, she wrapped her legs around my bald head, squeezing my cheeks. Wanting deep inside her, I fucked her with my tongue as a smashed my face into her sex like I was in a pie eating contest. I planned to win. My nose scrubbing against her clit, she came in no time, panting and squirming as she did.

"I told you it'd be quick," I said to her as I helped her down and back into her thong.

"Fuck. I'm sated but my knees are weak, you asshole," she joked, punching my arm. Reaching up she wiped at my mouth. Maren looked in my eyes like I hung the moon, but she said, "You'll need to wash your face. It's all shiny."

I licked my lips tasting her still there. "Maybe I won't until after the show. You'll be able to pick me out in the crowd that way."

"There's no way, I could miss you," Maren came in to give me a quick kiss until she realized I smelled of her pussy. "You might want to find a toothbrush too. I plan to kiss you properly later."

"I hope it's not just on my lips." I took her hand to run over the stiffness in my pants. "I'm going to have blue balls by the time your show's over."

"Meet you back at the house," she said, leaving for the stage.

"No, meet me at the funhouse."

Place had a thousand mirrors, and I wanted another show.

Morgan Jane Mitchell

CHAPTER 19

Levi

Royal Road's Haunted Carnival took on a whole new vibe once the sun set. Purple lights twinkled and strobes beat to Halloween sound effects of screams and screeching. The Ferris wheel was lit up. Two motorcycles roared as they flipped in the cage. A zombie Elvis ran around with a chainsaw, I hoped wasn't real. Smoke machines kept the outdoors coated in a creepy fog, but I went to the bar for a drink.

Inside it was pretty much the same Halloween party as always. Memphis inspected the strippers' killer clown costumes. Mainly their faces were painted, and they didn't wear much else but a few strategically placed pom poms. Though Leo had on the big clown shoes. Louise, short for Louisiana was laid out on the buffet, candy covering her naked body. She volunteered every year. Where the pool table had been, they'd set up a pit for Jell-O wrestling. Guess since they were using green Jell-O and called it slime wrestling, that was Halloweeny enough.

The crowd was in costume as usual, but this Halloween the bikers were too. Opry was a full-on cowboy, no surprise there. Gunn and Cricket our guards dressed as police officers but in retro uniforms with fake mustaches.

Pagan had on a red robe and slippers. I had to ask him who he was.

"Hugh Hefner," he said, showing me the bunny stuffed animal he cradled.

"With a beard?"

He scratched his untamed one. "If he was still alive, he'd probably have grown one by now."

"Riff sat at the bar in a top hat sort of like we gave Kingpin, but he was in a suit."

"Who are you supposed to be?"

He held an empty shot glass up to his eye. "The Monopoly man."

"Where's that nurse, Mary?" The one he said he'd be bringing to the party.

"She's helping Cece get dressed. Getting ready to meet her over under the tent. Watch that act of Maren's. We'll all be horny after it."

Paisley poured drinks as a fortune teller. Donning a long black wig, she'd gone all out in layers of colorful silk. She'd set the bar up like a séance, complete with a crystal ball and tarot cards.

"It's no fair you're not dressing up," she complained about me.

I'd gone home for a moment, washed my face and brushed my teeth, and that was all. I started to tell her to fuck off, but I thought better of it. In my cut, I stuck out like a sore thumb amongst my brothers. If the Gods did ambush us, I'd be an easy target.

"What would you suggest?"

"Let me think." Paisley held out her hand. "Let me read your palm."

"Pour me some whiskey first."

I played along and gave her my hand. Leaning over the bar, her breasts splayed onto the wood. It was a sight I used to love. But now all I could think of was Maren and what I planned to do to her if I got the chance tonight. Hopefully all this worry was for nothing. At least my brothers would be ready tomorrow if our enemies truly held off.

Running her fingers over it, tracing the lines, the whore studied my hand. It tickled.

"Hold still," she rumbled.

Her face screwed up.

"What does it say?"

"You're not going to be here much longer," Paisley announced, her eyes wide like it shocked her.

"Bull shit." I took my hand back. "Stop fucking with me."

"No, I'm serious." She shrugged. "You'll be gone tomorrow."

Chills ran over me, but I ignored them. I didn't believe in this spooky shit.

"I'll miss you."

"How about my costume?"

Paisley took off her purple sash and held it out to me. "Take off your shirt, vest, and that cap. Your jeans will have to do. Tie this around your waist" She rummaged under the bar. "An old man left this," she said, handing me an eye patch. "You're a pirate."

Groaning, I handed her my cut to keep behind the bar. Then I unbuttoned my flannel and took off my cap. Placing the eye patch on I felt absurd, but not as much so as I tied the scarf around my belt. I downed the whiskey and turned to leave.

"You're welcome," Paisley shouted after me.

"I'll thank you tomorrow," I shouted back. I didn't want to be late for Maren's show.

"You won't be here," Paisley yelled back.

Under the big top, the show had already begun, but just barely. Maren was just as beautiful as when I left her. The spotlight on her, she twinkled in the limelight. Her hoop had multiplied, and she swung between three swings. When she did, her ass showed as much as her tits bounced. Though I should be freezing, I was hot with anger. I didn't like all the eyes on her body.

I sat in the back looking ridiculous, hoping no one saw me.

Kingpin had a front row seat on his throne, his top hat on the woman in his lap. His pregnant Ol' Lady, Sky's belly paint had barely survived the party, the Jack-o-Lantern had half melted off.

I spotted Eve who refused to perform in a corner. Dressed in all black, she wore big black wings that looked way too big for her. Some women from the Eagle's Nest sat with her, a devil and a sexy firefighter. I'm sure I'd know them if I were to get closer. Maybe Connie and Allie?

Her ex, Hallow was across the room in a couple's costume with his ex, Steph. I knew the bitch well. She liked to ride motorcycles and smoke cigars. They were a Greek duo in togas.

Thorn sat with him dressed like a punk with his head actually shaved into a mohawk. No, with the big chains, I decided he was Mr. T. Beside him sat Villain dressed as Homelander, an evil superhero. It was fitting.

Irish hugged up on Cece. The Irishman was a pot of gold, and she was the rainbow. Fucking hilarious. If we had a contest they'd win. They had her new guide dog with them though, oddly dressed like a cheerleader that just didn't fit with their theme.

Riff sat beside the nurse he was after. She dressed just like an Amish girl, but sexy, a split up her skirt. The girl looked so old fashioned she really pulled it off. And that answered our questions about her.

Sweet Tea put her sexiness to shame, as Jessica Rabbit complete with ears. And I thought all the whores would be scary clowns tonight. I guess it was just the strippers.

Horror came as Gomez Adams and his girl Tonya, a corpse bride. Looked like there'd been some miscommunication. However, there wasn't a happier looking couple.

Cousin sat in two seats in an inflatable Stay Puft Marshmallow Man and whoever he was seeing was a lady Ghostbuster.

Payday, who I hadn't seen in a while came as a skeleton. His girl came as Carrie, from the movie, the prom queen, blood-soaked version.

Buzzard, Cue-ball, and Eight-ball and most of the older bikers took a page from Kingpin's book and didn't dress up at all. Fuck. Amongst them, I spotted the oldest of them all.

They broke out Satan from the nursing home for the celebration. Our ex-VP was going on one-hundred-years-old and didn't need to be here. Still in his hospital gown and slippers, he wore his old cut.

I slouched as a crude pirate, trying to watch Maren's show, but a whisper came from beside me.

"Nice outfit, Leviathan."

I looked over to get a shock, saw Holy and his girl Hazel, a priest, and his sexy nun. He held her neck by a rosary like she was his pet.

"What are you two doing here?" They were from the Charleston, West Virginia Chapter of the Royal Bastards MC.

"Fuck, we love Halloween."

That was all the explanation needed. Royal Road's party was known far and wide.

"We're not the only ones," Hazel peeped, but Holy yanked the necklace shutting her up.

Winking, he wasn't hiding nothing, just having some fun with his Ol' Lady.

"Yeah, it's not just us. More of us in costume. Opry sent an invite to the whole club," he said. "Said this was a surprise to cheer up your Prez."

Leaning sideways, I told him of the danger tonight.

Holy ran his hand up Hazel's thigh to show off the gun holstered there.

"We'll be ready at the first whiff of trouble. Love to kill me some Gods tonight. I'll be sure to let the others know."

Holy pointed out the other Royal Bastards he'd spoken to, but I didn't recognize right away because they were in costume like most of the large crowd.

It was no surprise the Memphis, Tennessee Chapter was here. Their Prez, Reign, a skeleton undertaker sat in the front behind Kingpin. His Enforcer, Country made as good a cowboy as our Opry did. Malice, Sergeant of Arms for that bunch pulled off Heath Ledger's Joker like no one's business.

Sitting with them were boys from Cleveland. Ghoul, their Prez came as Jason Voorhees. His Sergeant at Arms, Wiley made a great werewolf. Sleeper, wearing a pink tutu that about matched Maren's black one must've lost a bet tonight.

The Prez of Los Angeles, Capone, and his Ol' Lady, Danyella sat beside Kingpin's throne, dressed as a mafia prince and a dark queen. They motioned to Bear, their Sergeant at Arms, dressed as Zorro and a woman with him, Snow White while they stood at the tent's entrance searching for a seat.

All the way from Tonopah, Nevada's Chapter, their Prez had come, too. The Grim Reaper with his Ol' Lady, Trish, a sexy witch with a pointed black hat sat on the other side of my Prez. Beside them were Rael, their Sergeant at Arms, in black and white skull makeup as always and his Ol' Lady, Nylah who was pregnant like our Prez's Ol' Lady. That made her an even sexier, naughty nurse.

I sat up when the music changed to one of suspense. Maren balanced on one leg. Leaning back, her foot picked up a bow and held it in the air, showing it off as if she was a magician. Then she rolled back onto the swing, freeing both legs. With the other foot, she had a flaming arrow. Other performers joined her on stage. They twirled hoops of fire and threw flaming batons in the air while the suspense built. Maren aimed at a target. Using only her legs she shot the arrow across the stage, hitting the bullseye. The target went up in flames, but instantly disappeared. So did Maren in a puff of smoke. The crowd thundered. We stood and kept our applause. More than that, the bikers who all had a beer or a drink smashed their glass, celebrating.

Opry picked up a mic and announced from the floor. "The real Halloween party has begun. Enjoy our Haunted Carnival everyone."

Maren walked back on stage and took her bow. Someone threw flowers, and she caught them. Opry, that fucker. Hugging them to her face, she smiled big as she left the stage.

Before I left, I went and said hello to Payday.

"You using these?" I asked his girl dressed as Carrie about her prom flowers.

"No. Are you fixin to give them to the star of this show?" She guessed.

I nodded.

"Take them," she said.

Armed with a dozen white roses dripping in fake blood, I hurried to the haunted funhouse. I got there just in time to see Maren go inside. I stepped up and pulled the chain across the door so no one else would join us.

Inside I shouted for her, "Marco."

Her voice echoed, "Polo."

I followed her laugh through the maze of frightening figures. The jump scares didn't faze me. I found her in the hall of mirrors. Hundreds of her. Still in her sad clown make up and tutu, she was so fucking hot. I reached for her just to miss an illusion. Holding out my hands, I waited for Maren to come to me. Soon, the real Maren grabbed my arms.

"This room is freaky," she said, staring up at me. "And you're a pirate." She laughed at me.

"I'm here for the booty," I joked.

"Well, I did say I'd do anything if you worked that dunk tank."

"All I want is you."

"Are these for me?" Maren asked.

Marveling at her, I'd forgotten about the bouquet in my other hand. I handed them to her.

"Very frightening. I love them."

"I didn't get them. I'm not thoughtful like that. But you deserved something."

"You're all I want," she told me, dropping the flowers to the floor.

I bent to take her lips, tasting the bitterness of her black lipstick. But Maren was all sweetness as she clutched my shoulders. Standing on her talented toes, she returned my kiss like I'd expected her to before, full of passion, opening her mouth wide to let me enter. My tongue couldn't dip deep enough within her. I wanted to devour her. Seizing her cheek, I deepened our kiss. I found Maren's tongue in my mouth as enigmatic and breathtaking as her.

Draping my arms around her, if I could absorb her, she wouldn't be close enough. Her skin against mine, a drug I'd become addicted to, I drew her against my erection hard. My hands went everywhere, seeming to feel her all over at once.

Under the emotion of our embrace, Maren practically fainted into my strong arms. I held her limp body until I couldn't wait any longer.

I took her to the floor. Laying her down, I covered her with my flesh.

But she barely moved.

Fuck, she'd really passed out.

The room spun as I worried. As nimbly as I'd tied her corset, I undid it as quickly as I could. I tore it away. I thought I'd have to do CPR, but Maren sucked in a deep breath.

"I thought that only happened in the movies," she choked out. "You really took my breath away."

Relieved, I was also confused, and for a split second, I thought she'd died. I died for that split second as well. Gut wrenching, I never wanted to experience it again.

"I guess in the heat of the moment, I let you tie this corset too tight. I made it through the show but kissing like that had been too much."

"This was my fault?"

"I just need a moment," Maren said, breathing deeply.

On my elbow, I laid on my side beside her stroking her bare chest. She wore the silver pasties, but I planned to remove them as soon as she recovered. In nothing but them and the tutu, I understood I'd come looking for a booty call, but Maren was pure treasure.

Glaring at our reflection, I realized I still wore an eye patch. I took it off and flung it. A million versions of us surrounded me. Glancing up, we hung overhead as well. We looked alright together and what was more, we felt right.

Picking up her hand, I kissed it. "I've got a confession. I've thought all day you might betray me and call the Gods tonight to come kill us."

"Why would you think that?"

"Memphis said this whole carnival was your idea, and it got the wheels in my head spinning."

"It wasn't. Opry came to me."

"I knew I shouldn't believe her. But there's another reason. I planned to betray you and have you call them tonight."

Now Maren was perplexed.

"I know I told you to tell the Asphalt Gods you'd alert them tomorrow, but I was afraid you'd catch me unaware. I planned to scare you tonight and have you call them. But I never planned on hurting you."

"You were going to try and kill me?"

"Not actually."

"What did you think would happen to me when they came? One side would kill me," Maren said with a frown.

"I don't know what I thought when I made the plan, but I know now, I don't want to lose you. Maren, I want you to stay with me. I won't let anything happen to you. I promise. I want us, what we have, to be real."

Maren smiled and ran a finger along my jaw and that was all it took.

I dipped down to savor her lips again. With my eyes sideways, so I could watch in the mirror, my hand tugged the pasties off one by one. Without ending our kiss, I felt beneath her tutu and got my fingers in her thong. Yanking, I wrenched the fabric away completely.

Maren lay beneath me in just her black tutu and jewels. I petted the soft flesh between her thighs.

"Stop teasing me, Levi," she said into our kiss.

I dipped my fingers in her snatch and found her wet and ready. Maren went for my pants to unzip me, but the damn sash was in the way. She untied it instead. Pulling off the silk, she put it around my neck and tugged me back into a kiss.

As our mouths fought to know each other finally, I took care of my pants. I freed my erection and positioned myself between her knees. Spreading her legs wide, I butted my cock up against her juicy pussy. Knowing we'd worked her up to be able to really enjoy my size gave me such joy as I rocked my hips and stamped inside her.

Maren broke our kiss, calling out, the size of my dick still surprising her.

I stilled in her. "Say you belong to me, Treasure."

"What did you call me?" She laughed.

"You're my treasure. I've been looking for you all my life. I just didn't know it."

Maren beamed. "I'm yours, Levi. I've belonged to you since that first night I met you. Even if I thought you were a monster then."

"So, you'll stay here with me? Be my Ol' Lady someday."

"Are you asking me to marry you?"

"Eventually."

"I will, eventually."

"That settles it then. You're getting tattooed tonight. My property patch right over this pussy of mine."

"What about your wife? You'll have to promise to divorce her if I'm going to wear your brand on me."

"I will. Right away," I assured her. "How else are we going to get married. And tomorrow, you'll have to be off the property. I won't let anyone hurt you during the fight."

"Alright, what if your club finds out about me? What will you do then?"

"You're mine. You come first," I vowed with all my heart.

Maren bit both her lips. "I'm so happy I'm going to cry."

"Don't cry. I'm not done fucking you."

"Fuck me you big monster."

Attacking her, I rammed my dick into her tight twat, but this time, we kissed with all the love we felt for one another as our bodies moved.

As I pulled away, I wanted to tell her everything I felt. Maren had captured my heart. "I love you, my treasure."

"I love you too, my big monster."

My face hanging over hers, I fucked her at breakneck speed. I wasn't even tempted to look in the funhouse mirrors, Maren's painted face twisting in sheer delight was all that I needed.

Recovering on the floor, Maren's tiny frame laid completely on my large body. I did look in the glass marveling at her fine ass. Running my hand down her back, I stuck my finger in her ass crack.

"Don't you dare. I said no butt stuff tonight."

"How about tomorrow? You've not let me yet."

"If we survive this, I'll do anything," she said.

Although I wanted her again, Maren suggested we dress and go find our tattoo artist, Blitz, to give her a nice tiny property patch above her snatch. I thought I'd spied him here dressed like a vampire.

"I'm never going to dance bottomless anyway," she remarked as she pulled on her thong.

"Fuck, you're not going to wear that on stage if you're mine."

Maren punched me as I zipped my pants. It was the only stitch of clothes I wore out here and without her on top of me, I was nearly freezing.

"What do you mean if?" she asked with attitude.

I took her into my arms. "You are mine, treasure. Always."

203

"No matter what happens after we leave this funhouse?"

"Yes. Don't you trust me?"

"I do. It's just," she started.

"What are you worried about?"

"I don't know. I just have a bad feeling. No, I have to be honest."

"What's this about?" What was she lying about?

"You know how I told you about the ghosts?"

I didn't say anything. Yeah, I heard her speak about seeing things and hearing voices before. It made me worry for her.

"Well, one of them is warning me not to go outside."

"Like right now?" I asked her. Fuck, I loved her, but this was crazy talk. It reminded me of Paisley reading my palm, trying to tell me I wouldn't be here tomorrow.

Maren nodded. Unlike Paisley, she appeared frightened.

"As long as you didn't betray me there's nothing to worry about," I said, guiding her through the maze to the outside.

"I didn't," she assured me.

"Then nothing bad is going to happen to us."

I kissed her forehead.

Stepping out into the dark, I regretted my words because Killer stood in front of us. I'd recognize the leader of my adversaries anywhere with his long gray braid down his back and beard to match.

He held my daughter, Haven by the neck.

Morgan Jane Mitchell

CHAPTER 20

Levi

"What the fuck is going on here?" I asked, meeting Haven's watering eyes.

Killer pointed his gun at her head. But then he pointed his gun at me.

"Which one of you am I going to kill first?"

I held up my hands. "Killer. Let go of the girl."

If I rushed him, he could shoot her easily. I couldn't risk it.

"You mean, your daughter?"

"Killer, let go of my daughter."

He ignored me and focused on Maren.

"Good work," he said to her. He tossed Haven into Maren's arms. "You take care of the girl. I will take care of Leviathan."

I looked to Maren, but she wouldn't meet my gaze. She put her hand over Haven's mouth.

I died inside.

Killer said, "Maren. Or should I call you Spooky? You've earned your patch, girl. You will earn your backpack when you dispose of his spawn."

Maren said, "Yes, Sir."

She dragged Haven into the funhouse, and I couldn't believe my eyes.

Maren had betrayed me. My heart didn't just break, it exploded into a million pieces.

My daughter's life was on the line because of my mistake.

Killer said, "It's all over Leviathan. The Asphalt Gods are here, and we are going to wipe all you boys out." He glanced around. "I couldn't imagine my luck. I've already got a clubhouse here for when I moved back to Tennessee."

Killer wanted to get me talking, but all I could think about was my daughter. And about how Maren deceived me. How foolish I'd been. And I was going to lose my child because of it. If not my own life. Because I trusted Maren. I believed she loved a monster like me.

I didn't care about my life, but wanting to save Haven, I tackled Killer and took his gun, easily knocking him to the ground. The old biker came at me with a large rock. I took a blow to the head but still tried to fight as long as I could.

Maren

When we stepped out of the funhouse and saw the President of the Asphalt Gods MC of Arkansas, my President I was as shocked as Levi. I didn't know what the hell was going on. I had told the biker our plan was going down tomorrow just like Levi had told me to.

What was he doing here?

And what was worse, he had Levi's daughter by her neck. His weapon to her temple, he threatened her. I knew Levi would suspect me especially when Killer started praising my work. But when Killer pushed Haven into my arms, I had to play along or risk her young life.

Killer wanted me to dispose the girl. Straining my hand over her mouth, I shut her up. I dragged her into the funhouse.

I told her in a whisper, "You stay here, Haven. Do not say a word. I'm going to go save your dad. Hear me?"

Haven nodded her head. Then I let go of her mouth.

"I need you to go out of the back of this thing. Run as far as you can, through the woods. Get away from Royal Road for tonight. You hear me? You call your mom. You tell her to come and get you wherever you end up."

Tears in her eyes, she looked scared to death, but she nodded her head. I watched her run through the funhouse before I rushed back outside only to see Levi on the ground.

Killer pointed his gun at him.

He asked me, "What did you do with his kid?"

"I snapped her neck," I lied. "They'll find her in the funhouse. Won't that be amusing?"

Killer laughed as he cocked his pistol.

"Wait. Why don't you let me?"

Glancing over at me, he was curious. "This bastard really treat you that bad?"

"Oh, yes. This monster raped me every night for the last two weeks. I'd love to put a bullet in him."

"You poor thing. I really underestimated you. I didn't think you could pull this off. But then I got your text a couple of hours ago."

I felt for my phone, and I knew it was in the dressing room.

Who in the hell texted Killer with my phone?

"I was only in the area because we planned to do this tomorrow, but this is better, brilliant. With the chaos of this wild party, we're going to wipe all the Royal Bastards in Nashville out. I think you deserve to kill this one."

Killer handed me the weapon. "I always say ladies first."

Smiling, I took the gun from him and aimed it at Levi.

Killer said, "I have half a mind to let him live to find his daughter dead. But I'm not going to risk it."

"I don't blame you. He'd kill you all. He is a fucking monster," I said, trying to still convince him I was on his side.

Then I directed the gun at Killer. He couldn't even take a breath before I pulled the trigger and blew a hole in his chest. He collapsed beside Leviathan.

I fell too, trying to wake Levi.

He stirred, but just a little. He was groggy, but he was awake. Had he been listening all this time?

When he saw me, he growled, "You better run."

The man looked like he could kill me. And it wasn't at all fun. Levi thought I betrayed him. Though I hadn't. And if he was half conscious all this time, he would think I killed his daughter, too.

I was in true danger. And then I thought about the fact, Killer wasn't the only Asphalt Gods MC biker here. There would be a whole slew of them. A battle had began. Coming to, Leviathan began to rise up, looking more like a monster than I'd ever seen him. Dropping the gun so he could protect himself, I did just what he said, I ran.

Morgan Jane Mitchell

Levi

Coming to in the barn, hanging in between two shackles like a prisoner, I knew my time on this earth was limited. Kingpin stood in front of me. His sickened face bloody and beat.

"Leviathan, I can't believe you. I can't believe you didn't know that girl you were fucking was a goddamn spy. We found her phone. Something tells me that this is all your fault. I can't believe you didn't know."

I didn't say anything until I thought of Haven. "Is my daughter alive?"

"She is. But she's pretty shook up. Would you want your revenge so bad you would fuck around with a spy and not tell us? Put your kids in danger?"

"That's not what happened," I said, but knew it was true.

I'd fucked up, royally.

"Brother, you know me well enough to know, I can fucking tell when somebody is lying."

"What happened? Who did they kill?"

"Wouldn't you like to know? I say that's club business. And you're not part of this club no more."

"Just get it over with." I spoke of him killing me.

"Why you'd like that, wouldn't you? I know you'd love for me to murder you, put you out of your fucking misery. But I want you to beg. I want you to beg me not to kill your family once you're dead."

His glock hit my head.

"Kingpin, please. I know you too, fucker, and I know you wouldn't do that." I started crying.

"You don't know shit. You put the people I love in danger. Brothers have died because of you. Because you didn't put the club before yourself. Did you think Fireball wouldn't tell us that he told you about Maren being a spy weeks ago? That fucker haggled for his life."

"Prez, she tricked me," I said, my heart gone.

"You're gonna go and you're gonna bring me that fucking spy. We're gonna string her up like you always wanted. And if you don't come back, we're gonna send fifty men after you."

"What if I can't find her?"

"Then you're not coming back alive."

"What happens to my daughters?"

"I don't know Leviathan. I don't have those answers yet. I guess you better get your ass back here with the spy so we can answer them together."

Paisley was right. Staring down the barrel of my brothers' guns, I left Royal Road that night.

Three Months Later

I was sitting at the bar when she walked in. I'd recognize her anywhere. Although she dressed like a biker bitch. In a corner booth, I tugged my ballcap down, slouching so she couldn't see me. But I watched her as she ordered a strawberry margarita. She talked to the waitress. I've been coming here every week for the last few months waiting for her. And now I finally had her. I was going home.

Morgan Jane Mitchell

Maren

"You don't have to stay."

God, he was a good lay. But he didn't need to spend the night.

"No, really babe, I want to."

Why were these men all the same?

"Listen. We fucked and now I'm going to sleep. So, either take the couch or get out of here."

I liked my bed to myself.

The pretty boy climbed out of it in a huff.

"I don't know what I expected sleeping with a biker," he said, putting on his pants.

I wasn't just any biker. I was the President of my own damn club. I could have any man I wanted. But I didn't want just any man. I went to sleep and dreamed of Levi and what we could've had if things hadn't ended so poorly.

The next morning, I felt a warm, muscular body beside me.

"Richard, I thought you went home," I whined.

A massive hand clapped over my mouth. I couldn't scream. And something went lower. Something metal jabbed between my thighs. The man shoved something inside me, violating me. I opened my eyes to discover a bald head wrapped in black tentacle tattoos. A monster was in my bed. Was I still dreaming?

I heard the unmistakable noise of a gun cocking.

With his pistol pointed in my pussy, Leviathan hissed, "Did you miss me, Treasure?"

The End for Now.

Catch the exciting sequel in the new motorcycle club romance series,

Monster, Road Monsters MC

Enjoyed this story? Be sure to leave a review!

To read all about

Leviathan and Maren,

Opry and Leo

Hallow and Eve,

Kingpin and Sky,

Irish and Cece,

Pagan and Jassica

Riff and Mary

Thorn and Memphis

Horror and Tonya

Pick up the next installment of Royal Bastards MC: Nashville, TN

Morgan Jane Mitchell

PICK UP THE NEXT INSTALLMENT OF

ROYAL BASTARDS MC: NASHVILLE, TN

PAGAN'S X- MAS

From USA Today Bestselling Author Morgan Jane Mitchell comes the next installment of her Royal Bastards MC: Nashville, TN Chapter series, Pagan's X-Mas.

Pagan doesn't celebrate the holidays like his brothers, hence the name. He doesn't know if he believes in anything anymore. And this year the Vice President of the Royal Bastards MC in Nashville decides to leave his sister, Cece to her new man and his club behind altogether to escape to the mountains to the one thing he still believes in.

Jassica was not only Pagan's sister's live-in nurse, she'd been his side chic for years. His plaything. His secret. Fed up with the turmoil of their strange and unhealthy relationship, she left Royal Road just when the badass biker couldn't go look for her. He'd been injured in the fire. But now that he's healed enough to ride, Pagan is determined to convince Jassica to come back.

Snowed in with the biker, will Jassica change her mind about leaving this ruthless man?

Will Pagan finally let someone love the man behind his rough shell?

Morgan Jane Mitchell

CHAPTER – SURPRISE

Warning: Spoilers ahead for Valentine's Eve.

Deleted scene of Royal Surprise/ Chapter in Valentine's Eve

This is set before the end of the last book, Royal Surprise, before Sky is hurt, way before Halloween, as well.

Kingpin

I saw Eve after that night, the night I first found her in the basement. The night I took off my wedding ring.

That Friday night, she was to sing at Royal Road. I'd already kicked my Ol' Lady, Sky out of my life, telling her she'd be moving out of the Big House a couple of days ago. She'd been coming to the club and taunting me since. Flirting with other men, she showed me she was just who I thought she was, the girl who'd sleep with Ralph Getty of the goddamn mob before coming on to me.

Therefore, when Eve showed up, my mind had been elsewhere. On the fact Sky continued to make a damn sucker of me.

The pretty blonde knocked on my open office door and said, "I don't think I can go on."

My eyes narrowed. "Huh?"

Eve mangled her hands together like she always did when she was anxious. "I can't sing tonight."

Holy hell. I thought the girl might tell me she couldn't keep quiet about what had happened between us the other night.

"Shut the door," I instructed her.

I sat behind my desk so she couldn't see the raging hard on I'd instantly gotten thinking of our time together.

Eve leaned against the closed door. "Sorry. Opry said to let you know."

"Why not? Why can't you sing tonight?" I asked, harshly, almost pounding my fist on my desk.

I'd worked so hard coaching her, and we'd had an exceptional performance earlier in the week. Not the one in the bedroom, but the one on stage before this unfortunate business with Sky lying to me and the aftermath.

"I just can't." Eve tugged at the scarf covering her neck.

"Is this about… the bruises?" I sucked in my bottom lip.

"This scarf is hideous and yes, everyone knows about… my bruises. And about Hallow. What he did to me. I'm mortified." She wrenched the scarf off, revealing her colorful neck.

Fuck. I'd done that to her, and she'd loved every fucking second of it.

"At least they think he put them here," Eve said, knowingly.

"Eve," I warned at the mention of her talking about what we'd done.

My erection knocked against my leather pants, begging to come out. Not only were her bruises teasing me, reminding me of choking her while fucking her and her getting off so hard, Eve had revealed her subtle cleavage. Knowing what her tits tasted like, they called to me. I stood, though it was hard to. But I fought the urge to go to her and have her against the wall again.

"I'm not going to tell anyone." She stroked her neck. "It's between us." Her fingers carelessly ended up in her bosom for a moment as she went on, "I don't know what you think of me now. I'm not the type of girl that does something like that usually. I want to be mad at you, but I was in a bad place myself."

I noticed her engagement ring was as gone as mine. Had it been gone the other night? I hadn't cared or looked.

"You don't need to worry about what I think," I said.

She didn't want to know what I thought. I thought about fucking her again.

"This business with Hallow. What he did to you." I tried to focus on my anger at him, so I didn't lose my control with her.

"Everyone says you're going to kick him out or worse."

"What do you want me to do?"

She dipped her head and lifted a shoulder. "Don't. I think you already hurt him pretty bad."

"I did. I'd do it again. He deserves much worse." Anger rose in me just thinking of it.

"I agree, partly, but I can't be the reason for him getting kicked out."

"I can't make any promises." I wanted to kill him for hurting her. I wanted to hurt her myself but only to get her off.

"He's back with his ex." Eve pulled in her lips until they disappeared. Her eyes watered and she reached up to wipe one.

An urge settled in my loins.

Glancing down, she went on, "Not sure what that means for me. You said I can't leave the Royal Bastards MC. I'm not Hallow's anymore. Not sure what that makes me now, a club whore?" Her chuckle faded to a frown, "I don't know what to do about his damn tattoo."

Eve's sadness broke my heart again. But more than that, she was free, and I wanted to cut my mark into her. Take her for myself. I found myself in front of her, clutching the wall on either side of her.

"Eve, I won't let anything happen to you. I promise."

I'd gotten so close my beard grazed her nose.

She didn't pull away. Her brown eyes fluttered as she looked up at me. Her chest heaved between us. Fuck. What was she doing? Did she want me as much as I wanted her? I struggled not to press my erection against her body.

"Kingpin," she complained. Eve's dainty hands landed on my chest to push me away.

I didn't move an inch.

Inhaling, I smelled more than her sweet aroma, I smelled whisky. "You've been drinking?"

"So have you."

She could smell a half bottle of bourbon on my breath, too.

"Not as much as the other night," I admitted.

"We agreed that was a mistake. I'm not going to be treated like a whore."

I bent and my mouth went to her soft, blonde hair, her ear. I whispered, "You'll never be a whore as long as I'm around. But you do have to stay here at Royal Road. For your own protection."

"I can leave. I can go into hiding with my brother, Hob. No one will find us."

My hand dropped to the small of her back. "Fuck that. Don't leave me," I said, before I caught myself.

Eve sucked in a breath like she felt the panic behind my words. She didn't move her hands from me, but she wasn't pushing anymore. We were almost in an embrace.

I changed the subject. "Bring Hob here if he's in danger. You already promised him I'd protect him. Remember?"

"Where will I go? I can't stay in the basement hiding from the weirdos down there. I don't feel safe now that Hallow's been seen out with other women." Eve trembled.

I thought of Goliath's place. "You can stay in one of the houses out back until you make your way. So, I… the club can protect you. You can bring your brother here. Safer at Royal Road for him, too."

"I don't want to live with Hob. We were never really close. If he wasn't my brother, I'd not have any love for the guy."

"He can take a room upstairs, of course. You can live alone."

Her eyes squinting, she studied my face hanging over hers. "Why are you doing this for me?"

"I told you the club would protect you if Hallow won't. If you stay here, it'd be easier for you to perform, anyway," I reasoned, although I wouldn't give her a choice.

"I do need the money since I'm apparently single now. Are you doing this because of the other night? I don't expect you to help me because…." She couldn't say what we'd done.

My forehead touched hers. "What did we do, Eve?"

Her lips pursed into a pucker.

"Say it."

She rolled her eyes. "I reckon, you fucked me."

"I wasn't the only one doing the fucking, Eve. But no, I did more than that. Say what you said I was doing to you that night."

She looked away, sideways. "Oh, you buttered my biscuit."

That's what I wanted to hear.

My lips dropped to hers, and I devoured her honied mouth. Eve responded. Instantly, she reached up and snatched my long hair. Fuck. It was the other night all over again. Without breaking our kiss, I took her by the ass and got her to my desk. She spread her thighs wide, allowing me to step in close. Eve was wearing a white lace skirt, allowing me to press my dick that strained in my pants, right up against her wet panties.

Was this really happening again?

My hand went to feel the fabric between her legs. It was soaked with her desire for me. Directly, I unbuckled my belt, unbuttoned, and unzipped myself. Then taking my cock and my thumb, I moved her wet panties and was inside her warm cave before I knew what hit me.

I drew back from her kiss only a little to watch her reaction.

Eve gulped when I'd filled her to the brink again so quickly.

"I thought you said I wasn't a whore," she yelped.

"You're not." My hand went up her thigh, taking her clothes with it to her property patch. I dug my black nails in her tattooed flesh. "But my dick's in your pussy, making you mine all the same."

"Oh, Kingpin. I don't know about this. Sky was here in the club tonight."

"I sent her home. She's moving out for good. And call me Beau."

"But you're married, and there's no way…"

I didn't let her finish to know whether she was going to say there was no way she'd be with me.

"It doesn't matter. Your pussy is mine now." I shut her up with a kiss and my dick as I scratched at Hallow's name.

She writhed in pain as I scraped my nails across the tattoo, trying to tear off his mark.

Taking her hips, I yanked her forward further onto my shaft. Her arms around my neck, she broke our kiss and leaned her neck back. My face buried in her cleavage as I pounded her wet cunt. She cried out, and I put my hand over her mouth.

The music out in Royal Road thumped the walls. We could hear Dimple who'd taken over for her singing, "Mississippi Queen", and her guitarist, Rome shredding his guitar. However, I didn't want to take any chances. The bar sat just outside my office door. Boy, how I wish we were locked in my throne room where she could be as loud as she wanted.

I abruptly stopped and let go of her mouth.

"Next time you see me, don't wear any panties, you hear. Or I'll set your ass on fire again."

"Again?" she asked, falling right into my trap.

Lugging my dick out of her, I took her scarf off her shoulders and tied it around her mouth. Tied it on the back of her head, gagging her. Turning her, I pushed down her face first on my desk. I bent her over my desk. I yanked her panties up into her ass crack like a thong. One hand went to her back to hold her down as the other reared back to slap her ass.

She flinched.

My hold on her only grew.

"When you come to me, you need to be ready to take this dick," I said as I punished her.

Eve couldn't speak but was so tense. Caressing her cheeks, I ran my fingers down the crack of her ass. I stuck two digits between her folds, tickled her clit and felt her pussy moisten right in the palm of my hand.

She relaxed. I rewarded her by plugging her and stroking her textured walls.

"Good girl." I pulled my fingers out and up to my lips. I sucked them into my mouth.

Fuck, her pussy tasted divine.

Repeat.

I lit her ass a flame, spanking her and then rewarding her.

Eve hollered out into the scarf. My dick pulsated with every twitch of her body and muffled sound. Her muted screams spurred me on until her ass was bright red.

I turned her over and whispered in her ear. "I'll untie your mouth, but I'm going to gag you with this dick instead." I took my cock into my hands, stroking her pussy juices onto it. "I'm going to plunge this all the way down your pipes. Lay back, lean your head back," I instructed her.

Batting her wide eyes, Eve didn't fight it. Her head hung back over the desk, her chin up. I went around the desk and loosened the gag. Her sweet mouth opened and waited for my dick. The head slid between her soft lips, past her teeth.

"Make me come down your throat, and I'll make you come next."

Eve's mouth took a hold of my dick like a hoover. Fuck. I let her suck me a while, but still I wanted to deep throat her. I wanted to make her gag on my big dick. I took a hold of her bruised throat as I worked my long shaft past her tongue and down further. I was careful, but she couldn't move if she wanted to. The fact more than turned me on. Sweet, Eve swallowing my cock.

I didn't want to hurt her beautiful voice. Her pussy couldn't take all of me, but her throat sure did, for a single second at least before I released her and gave her a mouth full of hot cum. Eve swallowed all but a bit of it that escaped from the corner of her mouth. I scooped it up with my finger and held it to her lips. With a smirk, Eve stuck out her tongue as I fed it to her. My thumbs wiped her lips just spreading it.

Fuck. Eve looked so deliciously sexy eating my jizz. Just watching her submit to me had me ready to go again.

When she sat up, her hair was wild. I put it back behind her ears. "I'm going to come in you now," I said. Recalling our conversations before I felt it was safe to, but I asked. "Is that alright?"

"Again," she answered, her voice hoarse from having my dick in her throat.

I bit my lip. "Again. In your pussy this time. Would you like that?"

Eve nodded. She was worked up and wanted her own orgasm.

Taking Eve's hands, I led her to my leather couch. I sat and dragged her on to her knees on top of me. But I didn't get inside her right away. I undressed her until she wore nothing but her cowboy boots. I still wore all my clothes as I feasted on her flawless skin. With my eyes first. Eve was all softness and purity, not a mark on her but my bruise. Her property patch had a bloody welp on it. With my mouth I covered every inch of her until my mouth landed between her thighs. I drank from her again like I did the other night. I loved eating pussy, and Eve's pussy turned me on the most. Besides her softer than soft flesh it was how she stole my hair and tried to shove my head inside her.

By the time I'd edged my dick into her, she'd come already, but I expected her to again, for me.

And I wanted to blow my wad inside her sweet cunt. Eve wrapped her legs around me as she widened for my cock. I hovered over her on the couch.

"Beg me to come in you, Eve," I demanded.

"Why? I said you could."

"I'm all about consent. No. I want to hear how bad you want it."

"Come in me, Kingpin. Please."

"Not good enough. Tell Beau to come in his pussy."

"You want me to call you, Beau. I thought you hated that name."

"I'm taking it back. But just for us." I winked at her.

"Come in your pussy, Beau."

"Your pussy's mine now. Say it."

"Yes. My pussy belongs to you, Beau. Please. Now. Do it."

"Do what, baby?"

"Butter my biscuit, Beau."

We kissed like we were ravenous as our bodies melded into one wild being. I had to slap my hand over her mouth again as she came, screaming.

"I want you in my bed next time," I told her.

My dick burst inside her, erupting its warmth and goo. I felt it surround me as I pumped a few more times. When we were finished, I didn't pull out.

Holding myself over her, I told her, "I want you."

"Again?" she asked.

I'd meant I wanted her, period, not just having sex again, but I hesitated to explain.

"We can't go again. This has to stop." She pounded her fists on my chest. "You're married. And I'm not a whore. I just can't help it."

Eve started crying again.

"You're having a baby," she said. "With Sky."

She cried harder.

"Why can't we go back to just being friends?"

"We can't," I said. "We were never friends." Then I had to know. "Do you still love Hallow?"

"Of course," she said, breaking my heart.

"We won't do this again. This was a mistake," I said, my pride speaking, but my dick was still in her. I'd said she was mine. But her heart belonged to another man.

"You're right, Beau." Her hand caressed my beard. Eve looked disappointed for a moment. She was lying. She was just as torn as I was. What did she want from me?

From then on out, I tried my best to avoid Eve altogether as to not fuck her again.

I told Pagan to set her up in Goliath's place.

"Giving her one of the officer's houses?" he questioned me.

"It's the only way I could convince her to let this stuff with Hallow go. As in her not telling the authorities," I lied.

"What are we going to do to him? I mean, I saw what you did to him. You'd think that was your girl he hurt."

"With the fights on hold, Eve's been the only one around here bringing in the crowd lately. No one here spends money, no one eats, Pagan. You want to go back to running drugs for the mob?"

"Hell, no."

"I'd rather us earn our dirty money ourselves so that way we can keep it all."

"Gonna do anything else to Hallow?"

"Eve says not to."

"Damn. Okay. Maybe they'll get back together."

His words changed my mind about leaving Hallow be. "Put him in the barn for me, though. I'm not finished with him."

After a stiff drink, I grabbed my whip off the wall.

Out in the barn, Goliath sat in a human sized cage. He wasn't speaking to us. Having been in the slammer with him, I knew it'd take time to make him talk. I hadn't even tried to beat it out of him yet. We'd keep him fed and watered until he was ready to spill what him and Junebug had been up to with Ralph Getty.

Shirtless, Hallow hung by his arms between two chains. By the look of him, Pagan had opened the wounds on his face. Probably while trying to string the big guy up.

"What's this about now?" Hallow asked, drunk as can be.

I finished my smoke.

"About what you done to Eve. I ought to end you. I still might."

"I didn't do anything to her."

"You raped her."

"When?"

"Last month?"

Hallow looked confused. "Fuck. Did I? I was drunk, man. I really don't remember what happened, but I don't think I raped my fiancée."

"You don't even know?"

"Girl's always been willing even if I forced myself on her. Last time I saw her like that, in bed, we were still engaged. The very night you did this to my face. After it. Yeah, you told me to go to her. I did. I went to her, and we had it out."

"You admit it, then?"

"My heart's broken, man. You wouldn't understand. Maybe I did. It's fuzzy. Is that why she's not speaking to me?

I thought it was because I was with some other women that night."

"I'm not here to help."

"Why do you even care? Woman are raped here all the time. What makes Eve so special?"

Eve was special, but I wouldn't explain myself. I let out the whip and cracked it. "You're on probation until your back is healed."

"Go ahead. I'm so high, I won't even feel it."

"But I'll enjoy flogging you, pig. And don't worry. You'll feel it tomorrow when we leave you out here to sober up."

"You're only doing this because you're in love with Eve like everyone says."

Without another word, I went behind him. As I attacked his back, I knew I was in love with her. But I couldn't have her. I made Hallow feel my enormous pain. Feel my loss. Whatever Eve and I had going on was killing her, and I wouldn't hurt her.

For the continuation of this series, sign up for news
http://www.morganjanemitchell.com/join

www.morganjanemitchell.com

Morgan Jane Mitchell

ABOUT THE AUTHOR

Award winning, USA Today Bestselling Author Morgan Jane Mitchell spent years blogging politics and health trends before she rediscovered her love of writing fiction. Trading politicians for bloodsuckers of another kind, she's now the author of bestselling post-apocalyptic fantasy novel, Sanguis City. Her action-packed series of vampires, witches, demons and zombies is paranormal romance, dystopia, urban fantasy and erotica in one bite. When Morgan Jane is not creating the city of blood or conjuring up other supernatural tales, she's dreaming up erotic and dark romances including her latest bestselling erotic suspense, Asphalt Gods' MC series.

Morgan Jane Mitchell

READ MORE FROM MORGAN JANE MITCHELL

READING ORDER

Asphalt Gods' MC

SCAR

Seven Sunsets

Hell on Heelz (standalone)

Sunrise

Cowboy, Take Me

Picking Bones

Lucky Stars

Bone Daddy

Mud

Trax

Snakebite

Hawk

Freedom

Slayer (standalone)

Morgan Jane Mitchell

SPHALT GODS' MC SERIES
Scar, Asphalt Gods MC

Emery wants to die. Good thing she just ran into a killer. "They say what doesn't kill you makes you stronger, but that's bullshit. What doesn't kill you leaves a scar. More than the eyesore down my torso, I was a scar, the jagged, fucked up remains of a tragedy."

Scar's Nomad status gives him a chance to fulfill his one wish, but his lonely mission is interrupted when a possible one-night stand goes horribly wrong.

"They say what doesn't kill you makes you stronger, but what if I can't live with myself anymore?"

Finding the blonde face down in a puddle of her own blood jeopardizes everything. Saving her and keeping her quiet could get Scar killed, but when Emery wakes up, her shocking proposal for him to kill her starts the ride of his life.

Morgan Jane Mitchell

Hell on Heelz, an Asphalt Gods' MC novel

Morgan Jane Mitchell An Asphalt Gods' MC Novel. Full length, Stand Alone.

"They say time heals all wounds, but my time's done run out. I'm no spring chicken, but it's more than that. I've been mad as hell for far too long. It's made me a different woman, a bitter woman. No, they don't call me Rage for nothing—I'm a twisting bitch tornado and that's before you make me mad. When I'm not fuming, I'm secretly festering in suffocating smog of self-loathing. A man did this to me, and now that I've finally met another man, one who calms my storm, one I might let break through the thick thorny vines I've wrapped around my heart—I fear there's nothing left of me."

Edie Pearl better known as RAGE never thought her decision to leave her cheating husband and join the Hell on Heelz would land her as the potential President of the female outlaw motorcycle club when the Banshee is killed. Rage has spent the last two years mad as hell, nursing her broken heart with booze and fast men. When she's pitted against her fellow heel, Dixie, in a race to track down the Banshee's killer, she meets the man of her dreams. Mud may be the only man to get her motor running, but he's also her sworn enemy. Will Rage do the unthinkable and choose a man over her club? Or is time really up for her?

Mud's been a mess since his twin brother left the Asphalt Gods' MC. He'd hate to have to kill his own kin. When Scar shows Mud mercy by sparing his brother, he thinks everything will finally be back to normal. He's proven

Morgan Jane Mitchell

wrong. A ride to California is interrupted with by the Heelz. After he leaves his brothers and catches up to his enemy, he finds a beautiful woman, one he cannot resist. Him showing her the same mercy puts him in even more jeopardy. His heart on the line with his life, which road will he choose?

Cowboy, Take Me, Asphalt Gods' MC
Morgan Jane Mitchell

"I've been waiting all my life for a Cowboy." When Cowboy finds Halley outside of the Devil's Den, it's a damned dream come true for her, but she's not alright. With all the double-crossing going down within the Gods, Cowboy hides Scar's sister away until she's well and he can get a hold of Scar. He never expected to fall in love. When the two arrive in Tucson, they aren't alone, and Scar is beside himself.

Morgan Jane Mitchell

Picking Bones, Asphalt Gods' MC

Morgan Jane Mitchell

"Suzi was a bone. Like when I hunted one, a piece of my enemy, a substitute would not do… Nothing could satisfy me until I had her again…"

Can a one-night stand lead to a lifetime of love?

Bones heads to California not only to help Cowboy rescue the woman he loves, he's left something in Texas. Suzi has something that belongs to him. Not his heart. His unborn child means more to him than she can ever know.

Her life finally on track, Suzi doesn't want a thing to do with an outlaw, let alone to raise her baby around one.

Bones, not used to hearing no, does the unimaginable. At least Suzi couldn't imagine being kidnapped and hauled back to Louisiana, especially in her condition.

When they're done picking bones, will Suzi pick Bones?

Morgan Jane Mitchell

Bestselling Erotic Romance Table 21 Series In Too Deep (Table 21, Book #1) Morgan Jane Mitchell

25-year-old Loraine Wynters has always been in control. She takes what she wants, from a new man every night - and leaves. Too bad this has cost her last job and landed her in the local sex addict's support group where she is certain she doesn't belong. Within this group of weirdos, she sees a familiar face. Richard Mahoney may be the gorgeous 30-year-old, successful owner of Table 21, but he has lost more than Loraine could ever imagine because of his obsession. After learning all her secrets, Loraine's new boss Rick is determined to fix her with his own brand of therapy. After digging deeper, Loraine finds that her boss needs more than just physical healing. Can they repair each other so they can be with other people?

With both Loraine and Rick longing for a normal life, will a pact between them be the answer to both their problems? Or are they getting in too deep?

Morgan Jane Mitchell

Bestselling Paranormal Romance, Sanguis City Series Morgan Jane Mitchell

Ever wonder what happens after the world ends?

Lilanoir Rue did. A mere by product of the destruction, she never knew what had happened before hand either. Banished from the only place she called home, the Human Reservation, she wipes her tears and never looks back.

In a world gone dead, life has never been so good, for some. While others live in chaos, the chosen call Sanguis City home. The rich and powerful found a way to survive The End and to enjoy every minute of it, for eternity. On the brink of a gruesome death from starvation, disease or a hungry mutant, humans flock to sell their blood for peace.

The city of blood, made for and by vampires welcomes Noir, her kind are in high demand. Neither Human nor Vampire, Bleeders take care of the city in the daylight. Draining humans by day and dating Vampires at night leaves Noir little time to think about her past, or much else, until it finds her.

Printed in Great Britain
by Amazon